THE HOBBIT

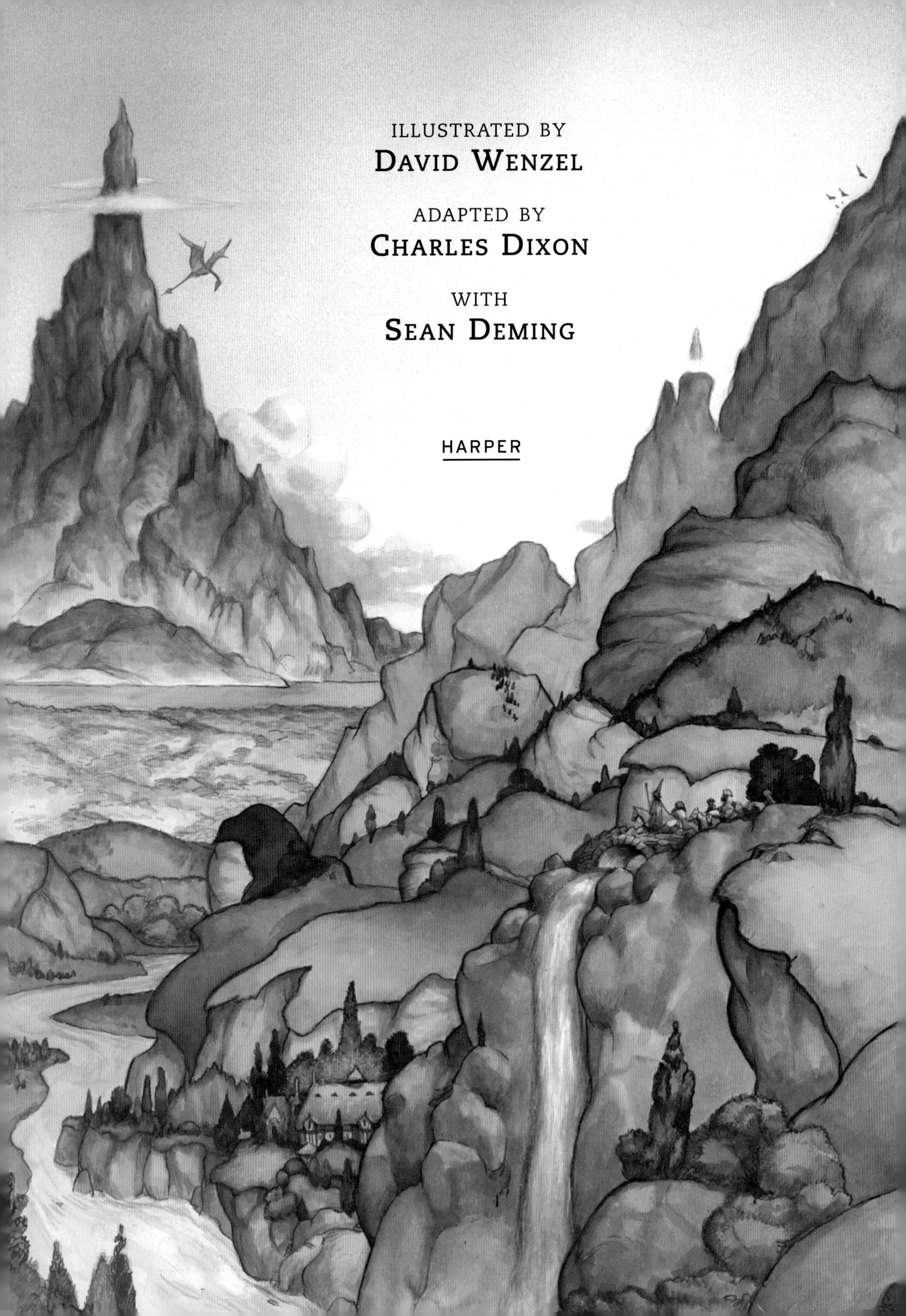

ILLUSTRATED BY
DAVID WENZEL

ADAPTED BY
CHARLES DIXON

WITH
SEAN DEMING

HARPER

THE
HOBBIT
OR
THERE AND BACK AGAIN
BY
J.R.R. TOLKIEN

HARPER

An imprint of HarperCollins*Publishers*
1 London Bridge Street, London SE1 9GF
www.tolkien.co.uk

Revised edition published by HarperCollins 2006
25

First published in Great Britain by Unwin Paperbacks 1990.
Originally published in the USA in three volumes by Eclipse Books 1989–1990.

This edition was entirely hand lettered by Bill Pearson. Hobbit logo by Steve Vance.
Revised edition designed by Terence Caven. Production by Anna Mitchelmore.

The Hobbit by J.R.R. Tolkien first published by George Allen & Unwin 1937.
Second edition 1951; Third edition 1966; Fourth edition 1978; Reset edition 1995.

ISBN-10 0-261-10266-4
ISBN-13 978-0-261-10266-8

Printed and bound by RR Donnelley APS

www.davidwenzel.com

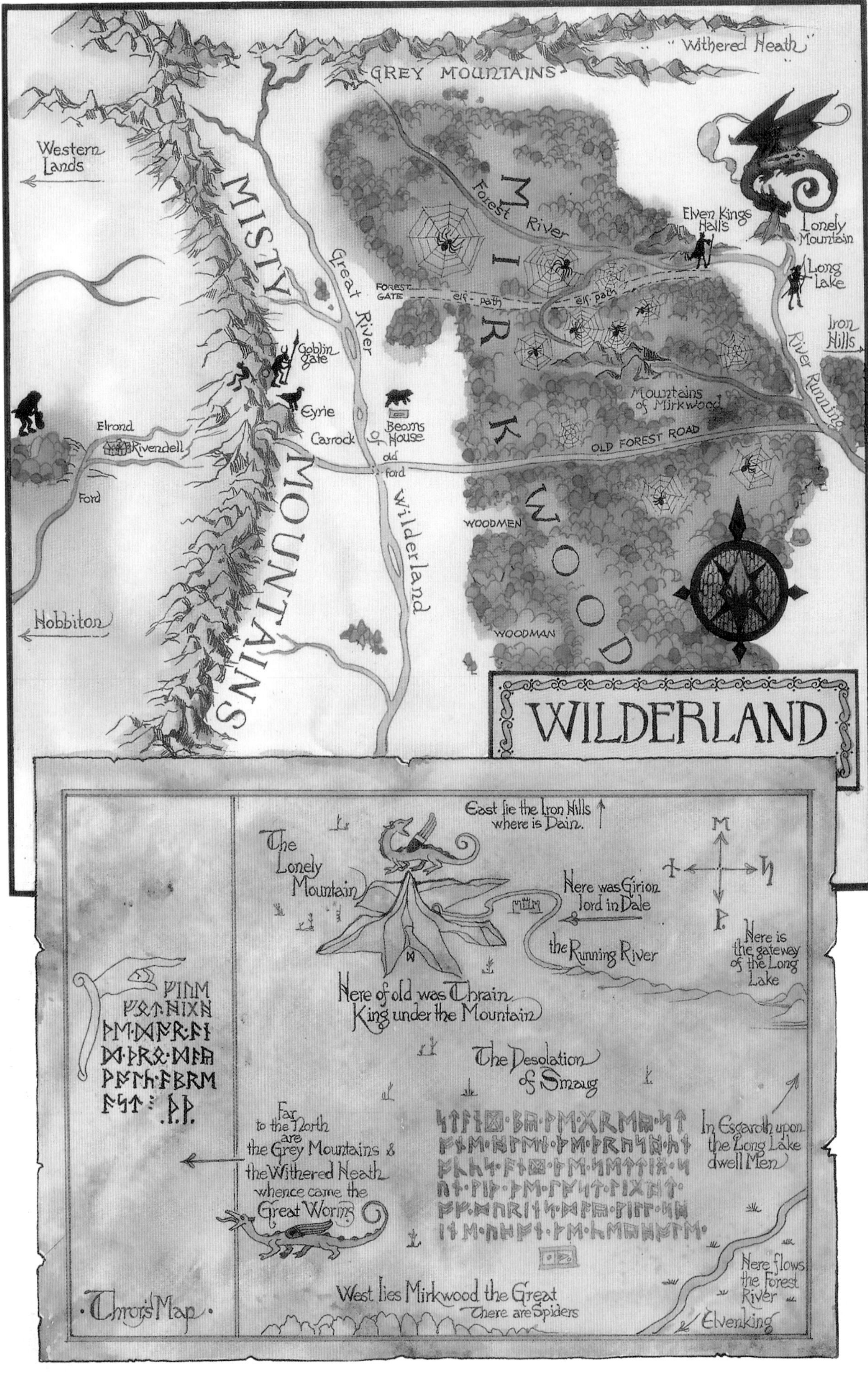

WILDERLAND
"Withered Heath"
GREY MOUNTAINS
Western Lands
MISTY MOUNTAINS
MIRKWOOD
Forest River
Elven Kings Halls
Lonely Mountain
Long Lake
Iron Hills
River Running
Great River
FOREST GATE
elf-path
Goblin Gate
Eyrie
Carrock
Beorns House
Mountains of Mirkwood
OLD FOREST ROAD
old ford
Elrond
Rivendell
Ford
wilderland
WOODMEN
WOODMAN
Hobbiton
East lie the Iron Hills where is Dain.
The Lonely Mountain
Here was Girion lord in Dale
the Running River
Here is the gateway of the Long Lake
Here of old was Thrain King under the Mountain
The Desolation of Smaug
Far to the North are the Grey Mountains & the Withered Heath whence came the Great Worms
In Esgaroth upon the Long Lake dwell Men
Here flows the Forest River
West lies Mirkwood the Great
There are Spiders
Elvenking
·Thror's Map·

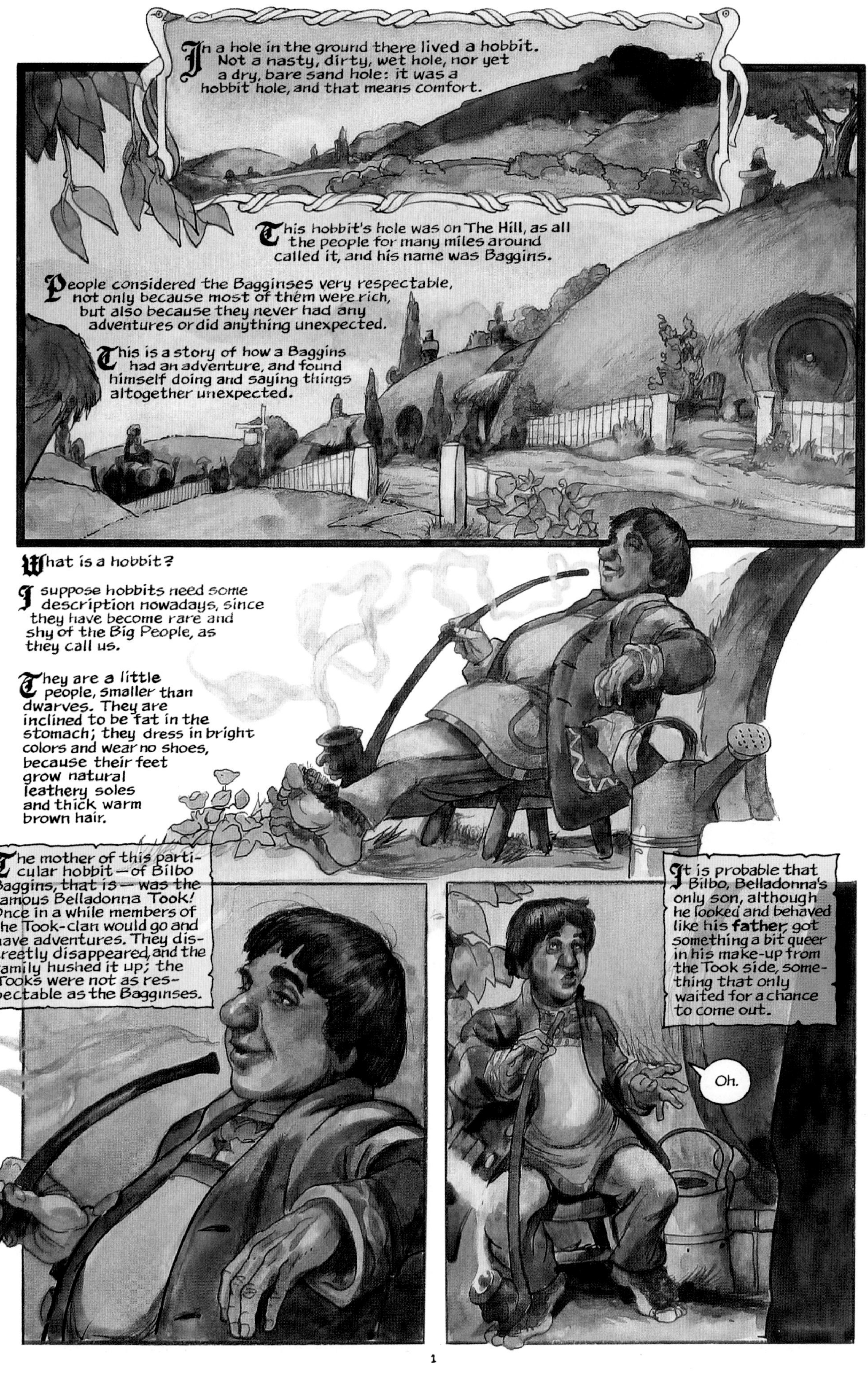
In a hole in the ground there lived a hobbit. Not a nasty, dirty, wet hole, nor yet a dry, bare sand hole: it was a hobbit hole, and that means comfort.
This hobbit's hole was on The Hill, as all the people for many miles around called it, and his name was Baggins.
People considered the Bagginses very respectable, not only because most of them were rich, but also because they never had any adventures or did anything unexpected.
This is a story of how a Baggins had an adventure, and found himself doing and saying things altogether unexpected.
What is a hobbit?
I suppose hobbits need some description nowadays, since they have become rare and shy of the Big People, as they call us.
They are a little people, smaller than dwarves. They are inclined to be fat in the stomach; they dress in bright colors and wear no shoes, because their feet grow natural leathery soles and thick warm brown hair.
The mother of this particular hobbit — of Bilbo Baggins, that is — was the famous Belladonna Took! Once in a while members of the Took-clan would go and have adventures. They discreetly disappeared, and the family hushed it up; the Tooks were not as respectable as the Bagginses.
It is probable that Bilbo, Belladonna's only son, although he looked and behaved like his father, got something a bit queer in his make-up from the Took side, something that only waited for a chance to come out.
Oh.

GOOD MORNING!
WHAT DO YOU MEAN? DO YOU WISH ME A GOOD MORNING, OR MEAN THAT IT IS A GOOD MORNING WHETHER I WANT IT OR NOT; OR THAT *YOU* FEEL GOOD THIS MORNING; OR THAT IT IS A MORNING TO BE GOOD ON?

ALL OF THEM AT ONCE.

AND A VERY FINE MORNING FOR A PIPE OF TOBACCO OUT OF DOORS. SIT DOWN AND HAVE A FILL OF MINE!

VERY PRETTY! BUT I HAVE NO TIME TO BLOW SMOKE RINGS THIS MORNING. I AM LOOKING FOR SOMEONE TO SHARE IN AN **ADVENTURE** AND IT'S VERY DIFFICULT TO FIND ANY-ONE.

I SHOULD THINK **SO** — IN THESE PARTS!

WE ARE PLAIN QUIET FOLK AND HAVE NO **USE** FOR ADVENTURES.

NASTY DISTURBING **UNCOMFORTABLE** THINGS! MAKE YOU LATE FOR **DINNER!**

GOOD MORNING! WE DON'T WANT ANY ADVENTURES HERE, THANK YOU!

WHAT A LOT OF THINGS YOU DO USE GOOD MORNING FOR!
NOW YOU MEAN THAT YOU WANT TO GET RID OF ME, AND THAT IT WON'T BE GOOD TILL I MOVE OFF.
NOT AT ALL, MY DEAR SIR! LET ME SEE, I DON'T THINK I KNOW YOUR NAME.
YES, YOU DO, BILBO BAGGINS, THOUGH YOU DON'T REMEMBER THAT I BELONG TO IT.
I AM GANDALF, AND GANDALF MEANS ME.
TO THINK I SHOULD HAVE LIVED TO BE GOOD-MORNINGED BY BELLADONNA TOOK'S SON, AS IF I WERE SELLING BUTTONS AT THE DOOR!
GANDALF! NOT THE WANDERING WIZARD WHO USED TO TELL SUCH WONDERFUL TALES AT PARTIES, ABOUT DRAGONS AND GOBLINS AND GIANTS AND PRINCESSES AND WIDOW'S SONS?
NOT THE GANDALF WHO WAS RESPONSIBLE FOR SO MANY QUIET LADS AND LASSES GOING OFF INTO THE BLUE FOR MAD ADVENTURES?
I AM PLEASED TO FIND YOU REMEMBER SOMETHING ABOUT ME.
I THOUGHT I WOULD SEND YOU ON THIS ADVENTURE.
VERY AMUSING FOR ME, VERY GOOD FOR YOU—AND PROFITABLE TOO, VERY LIKELY, IF YOU EVER GET OVER IT.
SORRY! I DON'T WANT ANY ADVENTURES, THANK YOU.
GOOD MORNING! BUT PLEASE COME TO TEA! WHY NOT TOMORROW? COME TOMORROW! GOOD BYE!

WHAT ON EARTH DID I ASK HIM TO TEA FOR?!

Heh
Heh
Heh Heh

SKRHITCH
SKRITCH

When tea-time came the next day, Bilbo had almost forgotten about Gandalf.
GOOD GRACIOUS ME! GANDALF!
DING-A-DING

DING-A-DING
DING-A-DING

I AM SO SORRY TO KEEP YOU—
—Oh!

BALIN AT YOUR SERVICE!
DWALIN AT YOUR SERVICE!
BILBO BAGGINS AT YOURS!
I AM JUST ABOUT TO TAKE TEA; PRAY COME AND HAVE SOME WITH ME.
MAY AS WELL LEAVE IT OPEN, MISTER BAGGINS.
THE OTHERS WILL BE ARRIVING SOON.
OTHERS?
DING-A-LING
GAN-DALF! SO YOU HAVE GOT HERE AT LAST!
KILI AT YOUR SERVICE!
AND FILI!
COME ALONG IN, AND HAVE SOME TEA!
DING-DONG-A-LING-DANG
SOME-ONE AT THE DOOR!
SOME FIVE I SHOULD SAY BY THE SOUND.
DORI AT YOUR SERVICE!
AND NORI!
AND ORI!
AND OIN!
AND GLOIN!

CAREFULLY! CAREFULLY! IT IS NOT LIKE YOU, BILBO, TO KEEP FRIENDS WAITING ON THE MAT, AND THEN OPEN THE DOOR LIKE A POP-GUN! LET ME INTRODUCE BIFUR, BOFUR, BOMBUR...
...AND ESPECIALLY *THORIN OAKENSHIELD!*

I AM TERRIBLY SORRY ABOUT ALL THIS. YOU SEE, THIS IS THE MOST AWKWARD WEDNESDAY I HAVE EVER HAD!
PRAY DON'T MENTION IT.
NOW WE ARE ALL HERE! QUITE A MERRY GATHERING!
I HOPE THERE IS SOMETHING FOR THE LATE-COMERS TO EAT AND DRINK!
Oh, DEAR! THE *TEA*!
HUSH! LET THORIN SPEAK!
PARDON ME.
GANDALF, DWARVES AND MISTER BAGGINS! WE ARE MET TOGETHER IN THE HOUSE OF OUR FRIEND AND FELLOW CONSPIRATOR, THIS MOST EXCELLENT AND AUDACIOUS HOBBIT.
MAY THE HAIR ON HIS TOES NEVER FALL OUT! ALL PRAISE TO HIS WINE AND ALE!
FELLOW CONSPIRATOR?

WE ARE MET TO DISCUSS OUR PLANS, OUR WAYS, MEANS, POLICY AND DEVICES. WE SHALL SOON BEFORE THE BREAK OF DAY START ON OUR LONG JOURNEY...

...A JOURNEY FROM WHICH SOME OF US MAY NEVER RETURN.

MAY NEVER RETURN ?!

WE HAVE LOST OUR HOST, I FEAR.

HUMPH! WILL HE DO, DO YOU THINK? AS SOON AS I CLAPPED EYES ON THE LITTLE FELLOW, I HAD MY DOUBTS.

HE LOOKS MORE LIKE A GROCER THAN A BURGLAR!

PARDON ME, DID YOU SAY "BURGLAR" ?

YES. I WAS TALKING ABOUT **YOU.** GANDALF TOLD US THAT THERE WAS A BURGLAR IN THESE PARTS LOOKING FOR A **JOB** AT ONCE, AND THAT HE HAD ARRANGED FOR A MEETING HERE THIS WEDNESDAY TEA-TIME.

THERE IS THE MARK ON YOUR DOOR— THE USUAL ONE IN THE TRADE, OR USED TO BE— **BURGLAR WANTS A GOOD JOB, PLENTY OF EXCITEMENT AND REASONABLE REWARD.**

BURGLAR ?

YOU CAN SAY **EXPERT TREASURE HUNTER** IF YOU LIKE. IT'S ALL THE SAME TO US.

LET'S HAVE NO MORE ARGUMENT. IF I SAY MISTER BAGGINS IS A BURGLAR, A BURGLAR HE IS, OR WILL BE WHEN THE TIME COMES. THERE IS A LOT MORE IN HIM THAN YOU GUESS, AND A DEAL MORE THAN HE HAS ANY IDEA OF HIMSELF.

NOW, BILBO, MY BOY, FETCH THE LAMP, AND LET'S HAVE A LITTLE LIGHT ON...

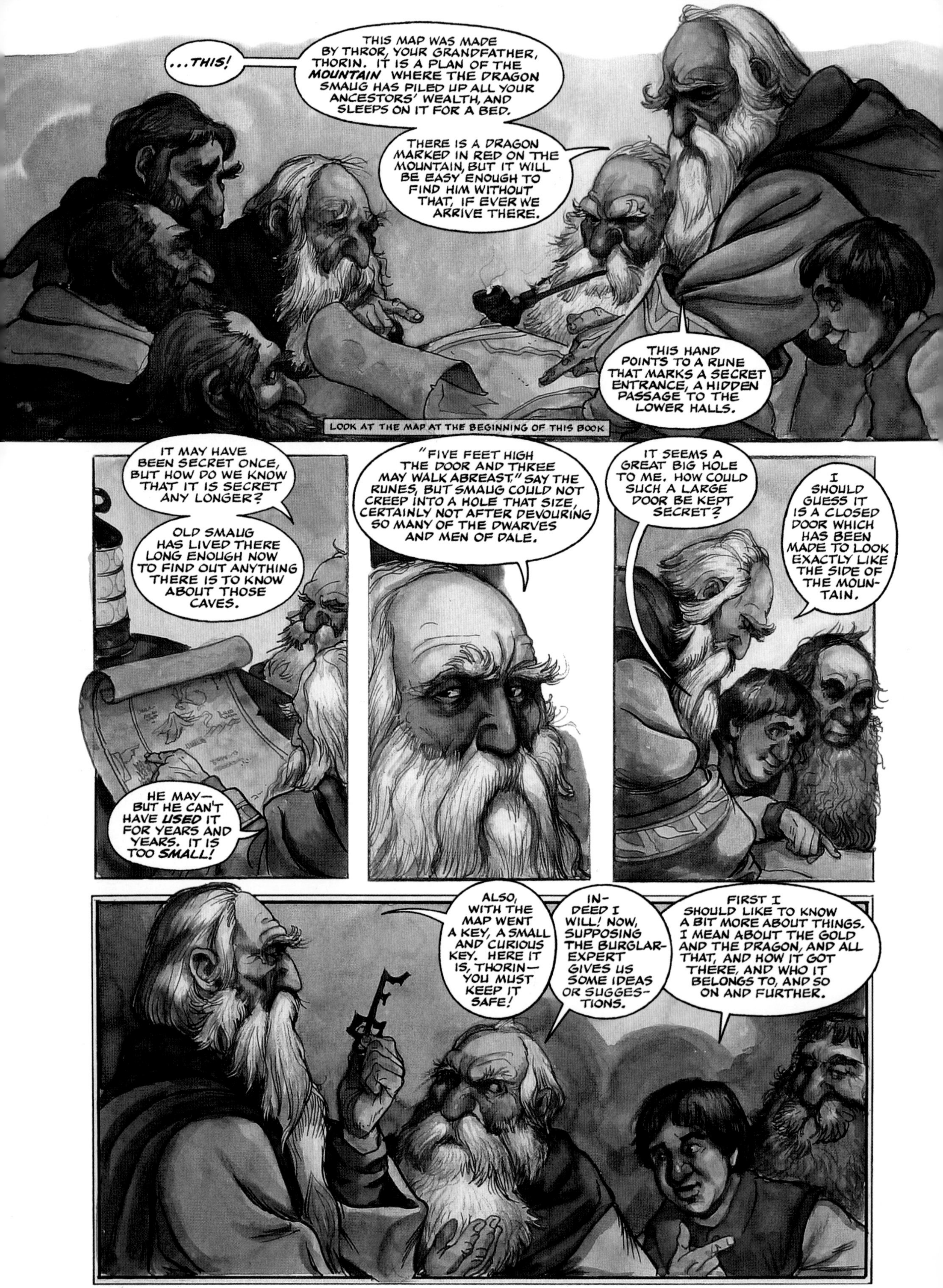

...THIS!
THIS MAP WAS MADE BY THROR, YOUR GRANDFATHER, THORIN. IT IS A PLAN OF THE **MOUNTAIN** WHERE THE DRAGON SMAUG HAS PILED UP ALL YOUR ANCESTORS' WEALTH, AND SLEEPS ON IT FOR A BED.
THERE IS A DRAGON MARKED IN RED ON THE MOUNTAIN, BUT IT WILL BE EASY ENOUGH TO FIND HIM WITHOUT THAT, IF EVER WE ARRIVE THERE.
THIS HAND POINTS TO A RUNE THAT MARKS A SECRET ENTRANCE, A HIDDEN PASSAGE TO THE LOWER HALLS.

LOOK AT THE MAP AT THE BEGINNING OF THIS BOOK

IT MAY HAVE BEEN SECRET ONCE, BUT HOW DO WE KNOW THAT IT IS SECRET ANY LONGER?
OLD SMAUG HAS LIVED THERE LONG ENOUGH NOW TO FIND OUT ANYTHING THERE IS TO KNOW ABOUT THOSE CAVES.
HE MAY—BUT HE CAN'T HAVE **USED** IT FOR YEARS AND YEARS. IT IS TOO **SMALL!**

"FIVE FEET HIGH THE DOOR AND THREE MAY WALK ABREAST," SAY THE RUNES, BUT SMAUG COULD NOT CREEP INTO A HOLE THAT SIZE, CERTAINLY NOT AFTER DEVOURING SO MANY OF THE DWARVES AND MEN OF DALE.

IT SEEMS A GREAT BIG HOLE TO ME. HOW COULD SUCH A LARGE DOOR BE KEPT SECRET?
I SHOULD GUESS IT IS A CLOSED DOOR WHICH HAS BEEN MADE TO LOOK EXACTLY LIKE THE SIDE OF THE MOUN-TAIN.

ALSO, WITH THE MAP WENT A KEY, A SMALL AND CURIOUS KEY. HERE IT IS, THORIN—YOU MUST KEEP IT SAFE!
IN-DEED I WILL! NOW, SUPPOSING THE BURGLAR-EXPERT GIVES US SOME IDEAS OR SUGGES-TIONS.
FIRST I SHOULD LIKE TO KNOW A BIT MORE ABOUT THINGS. I MEAN ABOUT THE GOLD AND THE DRAGON, AND ALL THAT, AND HOW IT GOT THERE, AND WHO IT BELONGS TO, AND SO ON AND FURTHER.

LONG AGO IN MY GRANDFATHER THROR'S TIME OUR FAMILY WAS DRIVEN OUT OF THE FAR NORTH, AND CAME BACK WITH ALL THEIR WEALTH AND TOOLS TO THIS MOUNTAIN ON THE MAP.
IT HAD BEEN DISCOVERED BY MY FAR ANCESTOR, THRAIN THE OLD, BUT NOW THEY MINED AND THEY MADE HUGER HALLS— AND I BELIEVE THEY FOUND A GOOD DEAL OF GOLD AND A GREAT MANY JEWELS TOO.
ANYWAY THEY GREW IMMENSELY RICH AND FAMOUS, AND MY GRANDFATHER WAS **KING UNDER THE MOUNTAIN** AGAIN.
WE TRADED WITH THE MORTAL MEN OF DALE AND THOSE WHO LIVED SOUTH ALONG THE RUNNING RIVER. SO MY GRANDFATHER'S HALLS BECAME FULL OF ARMOUR AND JEWELS AND CARVINGS AND CUPS.
UNDOUBTEDLY THAT WAS WHAT BROUGHT THE DRAGON. DRAGONS STEAL GOLD AND JEWELS WHEREVER THEY CAN FIND THEM; AND THEY GUARD THEIR PLUNDER AS LONG AS THEY LIVE (WHICH IS PRACTICALLY FOREVER), AND NEVER ENJOY IT AT ALL.
ONE DAY AN ESPECIALLY GREEDY, STRONG AND WICKED WORM CALLED SMAUG CAME OUT OF THE NORTH. DALE WAS RUINED AND SMAUG DROVE US FROM THE MOUNTAIN AND TOOK THE TREASURE OF MY ANCESTORS FOR HIS OWN.
WE STILL MEAN TO GET IT BACK, AND TO BRING OUR CURSES HOME TO SMAUG— IF WE CAN.

I SEE NOW MY FATHER AND GRAND-FATHER MUST HAVE ESCAPED THROUGH THE HIDDEN SIDE-DOOR, BUT I SHOULD LIKE TO KNOW HOW GANDALF GOT HOLD OF THIS MAP, AND WHY IT DID NOT COME DOWN TO ME, THE RIGHTFUL HEIR.
I DID NOT "GET HOLD OF IT," I WAS GIVEN IT. YOUR GRANDFATHER THROR WAS KILLED, YOU REMEMBER, IN THE MINES OF MORIA BY AZOG THE GOBLIN.
AND THRAIN YOUR FATHER WENT AWAY A HUNDRED YEARS AGO AND HAS NEVER BEEN SEEN BY YOU SINCE.
WELL, YOUR FATHER GAVE ME THIS TO GIVE TO YOU. HOW HE GOT THERE I DON'T KNOW, BUT I FOUND HIM A PRISONER IN THE DUNGEONS OF THE NECROMANCER. I TRIED TO SAVE HIM, BUT IT WAS TOO LATE!
HE WAS WITLESS AND WANDERING, AND HAD FORGOTTEN EVERYTHING EXCEPT THE MAP AND THE KEY. A NASTY, DANGEROUS BUSINESS IT WAS. EVEN I, GANDALF, ONLY JUST ESCAPED.
WELL, I SHOULD SAY YOU OUGHT TO GO EAST AND HAVE A LOOK AROUND. AFTER ALL, THERE IS THE SIDE-DOOR, AND DRAGONS MUST SLEEP SOMETIMES, I SUPPOSE.
IF YOU SIT ON THE DOOR-STEP LONG ENOUGH, I DARESAY YOU WILL THINK OF SOMETHING.
WE WILL THINK OF SOMETHING, I SUPPOSE YOU MEAN.
AND ISN'T SITTING ON THE DOOR-STEP THE BURGLAR'S JOB, NOT TO SPEAK OF GETTING INSIDE THE DOOR?
I SUPPOSE.
THEN IT IS DECIDED! WE SHALL RECLAIM OUR ANCESTORS' TREASURE WHICH WAS STOLEN BY THAT FOUL WORM SMAUG.
FAR OVER THE MISTY MOUNTAINS COLD
TO DUNGEONS DEEP AND CAVERNS OLD
WE MUST AWAY, ERE BREAK OF DAY
TO CLAIM OUR LONG-FORGOTTEN GOLD.
oh, DEAR

The next morning when he awoke, Bilbo was really relieved to find the dwarves had all gone on without him; and yet in a way he could not help feeling just a trifle disappointed. The feeling surprised him.
DON'T BE A FOOL, BILBO BAGGINS! THINKING OF DRAGONS AND ALL THAT OUTLANDISH NONSENSE AT YOUR AGE!

MY DEAR FELLOW, IT'S HALF PAST TEN! WHENEVER ARE YOU GOING TO COME? THEY LEFT YOU THE MESSAGE BECAUSE THEY COULD NOT WAIT.
WHAT MESSAGE?
GREAT ELEPHANTS! YOU ARE NOT AT ALL YOURSELF THIS MORNING. IF YOU HAD DUSTED THE MANTLEPIECE, YOU WOULD HAVE FOUND THIS JUST UNDER THE CLOCK.
THORÏN AND COMPANY TO BURGLAR BÏLBO GREETINGS!
FOR YOUR OFFER OF PROFESSÏONAL ASSÏSTANCE OUR GRATEFUL ACCEPTANCE.
TERMS: CASH ON DELIVERY UP TO AND NOT EXCEEDING ONE FOURTEENTH OF TOTAL PROFITS (IF ANY); ALL TRAVELING EXPENSES GUARANTEED ÏN ANY EVENT FUNERAL EXPENSES TO BE DEFRAYED BY US OR OUR REPRESENTATÏVES, IF OCCASION ARISES.
WE HAVE PROCEEDED ÏN ADVANCE TO MAKE REQUÏSITE PREPARATÏONS, AND SHALL AWAIT YOUR RESPECTED PERSON AT THE GREEN DRAGON INN, BYWATER, AT 11:00 A.M. SHARP.
WE HAVE THE HONOR TO REMAIN YOURS DEEPLY—
THORIN & COMPANY

THAT LEAVES YOU JUST TEN MINUTES. YOU WILL HAVE TO RUN.
BUT-

NO TIME FOR IT.
BUT-

NO TIME FOR THAT EITHER!

OFF YOU GO!

That is how they all came to start, jogging off from the inn one fine morning just before May.
The party went along very merrily, and they told stories or sang songs as they rode forward.
Bilbo began to feel that adventures were not so bad after all.
At first they passed through hobbit-lands, a wild, respectable country inhabited by decent folk.
Then they came to lands where people spoke strangely, and sang songs Bilbo had never heard before.
They passed through the Lone-lands, where there were no people left, no inns, and the roads grew steadily worse.
Now they climbed up dreary hills, rising higher and higher.
Everything seemed gloomy, for the weather that had mostly been as good as May can be had taken a nasty turn.
TO THINK IT WILL SOON BE JUNE. I'M SURE THE RAIN HAS GOTTEN INTO THE DRY CLOTHES AND THE FOODBAGS.
WHAT LANDS ARE THESE, THORIN?
THESE PARTS ARE NONE TOO WELL KNOWN, AND ARE TOO NEAR THE MOUNTAINS.
THE OLD MAPS ARE NO USE: THINGS HAVE CHANGED FOR THE WORSE. BUT THIS PLACE IS AS DRY AS ANY. WE WILL CAMP HERE.

LET ME TRY, GLOIN.
YOU'VE ALREADY TRIED TO LIGHT THE FIRE, OIN, AND FARED NO BETTER.
OH, BOTHER BURGLING AND EVERYTHING TO DO WITH IT! I WISH I WAS AT HOME IN MY NICE LITTLE HOLE BY THE FIRE, WITH THE KETTLE JUST BEGINNING TO SING!
I ONLY WONDER WHERE HAS GANDALF GOT TO?
JUST WHEN A WIZARD WOULD HAVE BEEN MOST USEFUL, TOO.
THERE'S A LIGHT OVER THERE!
WHERE?
JUST THERE. SEE THE GLOW?
COULD IT BE A TRAVELER?
NO ONE TRAVELS THESE WICKED LANDS.
THERE ARE FOURTEEN OF US.
WHERE HAS GANDALF GOT TO?
SEND THE BURGLAR!
THE BURGLAR!
YOU MUST GO ON AND FIND OUT ALL ABOUT THAT LIGHT.
NOW SCUTTLE OFF, AND COME BACK QUICK, IF ALL IS WELL. IF NOT, COME BACK IF YOU CAN!
IF YOU CAN'T, HOOT TWICE LIKE A BARN-OWL, AND ONCE LIKE A SCREECH-OWL, AND WE WILL DO WHAT WE CAN.
Oh, DEAR.
I CANNOT HOOT EVEN ONCE LIKE ANY KIND OF OWL ANY MORE THAN FLY LIKE A BAT.

MUTTON YESTERDAY, MUTTON TODAY, AND BLIMEY, IF IT DON'T LOOK LIKE MUTTON AGAIN TOMORRER.
TROLLS.

YOU'VE ET A VILLAGE AND A HALF BETWEEN YER, SINCE WE COME DOWN FROM THE MOUNTAINS. HOW MUCH MORE D'YER WANT?
OW!
A really first-class burglar would at this point have picked the trolls' pockets — it is nearly always worthwhile, if you can manage it. Others would perhaps have stuck a dagger into each of them before they observed it. Then the night could have been spent cheerily.
AND TIME'S BEEN UP OUR WAY, WHEN YER'D HAVE SAID THANK YER BILL, FOR A NICE BIT O' FAT VALLEY MUTTON LIKE WHAT THIS IS.
Bilbo knew it. He had read of a good many things he had never seen or done. He wished himself a hundred miles away, and yet— and yet somehow he could not go straight back to Thorin and Company empty-handed.
'ERE, 'OO ARE YOU?
Oh!
BLIMEY, BERT, LOOK WHAT I'VE COPPED!
WHAT IS IT?
LUMME, IF I KNOWS!

WHAT ARE YER?
BILBO BAGGINS, A BUR-A HOBBIT.
A BURRAHOBBIT? WHAT'S A BURRAHOBBIT GOT TO DO WITH MY POCKET ANYWAYS?
AND CAN YER COOK 'EM?
YER CAN TRY. P'RAPS THERE ARE MORE LIKE HIM ROUND ABOUT, AND WE MIGHT MAKE A PIE.
HERE YOU, ARE THERE ANY MORE OF YOUR SORT A-SNEAKIN' IN THESE HERE WOODS, YER NASSTY LITTLE RABBIT?
YES, LOTS.
NO, NOT AT ALL, NOT ONE!
WHAT D'YER MEAN?
POOR LITTLE BLIGHTER! LET HIM GO! I'VE 'AD ME SUPPER ANYWAY!
NOT TILL HE SAYS WHAT HE MEANS BY LOTS AND NONE AT ALL.
I DON'T WANT TO HAVE ME THROAT CUT IN ME SLEEP!
HOLD HIS TOES IN THE FIRE TILL HE TALKS!
I WON'T HAVE IT. I CAUGHT HIM ANY-WAY!
YOU'RE A FAT FOOL, WILLIAM, AS I'VE SAID AFORE THIS EVENING.
AND YOU'RE A LOUT!
AND I WON'T TAKE THAT FROM YOU, BILL HUGGINS!

BILBO! WHAT. . .
BALIN!

A DWARF!
AN *UNCOOKED* DWARF!
A SACK, TOM, QUICK!

THERE'S MORE TO COME YET, OR I'M MIGHTY MISTOOK. LOTS AND NONE AT ALL, IT IS. NO BURRAHOBBITS, BUT LOTS OF THESE HERE *DWARVES!*
I RECKON YOU'RE RIGHT AND WE'D BEST GET OUT OF THE LIGHT.

OIN? GLOIN?
And so they did. As each dwarf came up and looked at the fire, and the spilled jugs, and the gnawed mutton, in surprise, pop! went a nasty smelly sack over his head, and he was down.

THAT'LL TEACH 'EM.
WHAT'S ALL THIS TROUBLE? WHO HAS BEEN KNOCKING MY PEOPLE ABOUT?
IT'S *TROLLS!* THEY'RE HIDING IN THE BUSHES WITH SACKS.
O! *ARE* THEY?

ARRRRRRR
PSSSH
THAT LAST ONE 'URT ME IN ME EYE.
SO WE ROAST 'EM NOW! THEN WE CARRY 'EM OFF TO EAT LATER!
NO GOOD ROASTING 'EM NOW, IT'D TAKE ALL NIGHT.
DON'T START THE ARGUING ALL OVER AGAIN OR IT WILL TAKE ALL NIGHT.
WHO'S A-ARGUING?
YOU ARE.
YOU'RE A LIAR.
AND YOU'RE A BOOBY.
WHY DON'T WE MINCE 'EM FINE AND BOIL 'EM?
NO GOOD BOILING 'EM! WE AIN'T GOT NO WATER, AND IT'S A LONG WAY TO THE WELL AND ALL.
SHUT UP! OR WE'LL NEVER HAVE DONE. AND YER CAN FETCH THE WATER YERSELF, IF YER SAY ANY MORE.
SHUT UP YER-SELF!
WHO'S ARGUING BUT YOU, I'D LIKE TO KNOW.

NOW STOP IT! THE NIGHT'S GETTIN' ON, AND DAWN COMES EARLY. LET'S GET ON WITH IT!
DAWN TAKE YOU ALL...
...AND BE...
...STONE TO YOU!
EXCELLENT!
GANDALF! IT WAS YOUR VOICE THAT GOT THE TROLLS TO ARGUE!
INDEED! YOU SEE, TROLLS MUST BE UNDERGROUND BEFORE DAWN OR THEY GO BACK TO THE STUFF OF THE MOUNTAINS THEY ARE MADE OF AND NEVER MOVE AGAIN.
BUT AS TROLLS ARE SLOW, AND DAWN WAS NOT FAR OFF, IT WAS A SIMPLE THING TO KEEP THEM BICKERING AND QUARRELING, UNTIL THE LIGHT CAME AND MADE AN END OF THEM.
The dwarves had to hear Bilbo's account of what happened to him twice over, before they were satisfied.
...AND BEFORE I COULD GET AWAY, HE HAD GRABBED ME BY THE NECK.
SILLY TIME TO GO PRACTISING PINCHING AND POCKET-PICKING, WHEN WHAT WE WANTED WAS FIRE AND FOOD!
AND THAT'S JUST WHAT YOU WOULDN'T HAVE GOT IN ANY CASE. ANYHOW, YOU ARE WASTING TIME NOW!
DON'T YOU REALIZE THAT THE TROLLS MUST HAVE A CAVE OR A HOLE DUG SOMEWHERE NEAR TO HIDE FROM THE SUN IN? WE MUST LOOK INTO IT!

HERE ARE SOME TROLL-PRINTS LEADING BACK THROUGH THE TREES!
PERHAPS THEIR CAVE LIES AT THE END.

They followed the tracks up the hill, until they came on a big door of stone leading to a cave. But they could not open it, not though they all pushed, while Gandalf tried various incantations.

WOULD THIS BE ANY GOOD? I FOUND IT ON THE GROUND WHERE THE TROLLS HAD THEIR FIGHT.

WHY ON EARTH DIDN'T YOU MENTION IT BEFORE?
NOW TO SEE WHAT TREASURES A ***TROLL*** HOARDS.

THIS PLACE ***SMELLS*** OF TROLLS.
AND NO WONDER.
CARRY THE GOLD OUTSIDE. WE'LL ***BURY*** IT FOR OUR RETURN TRIP.
TAKE ANY FOOD THAT HASN'T ROTTED.

THESE LOOK LIKE GOOD BLADES.

THEY WERE NOT MADE BY ANY TROLL, NOR ANY SMITH AMONG MEN IN THESE PARTS AND DAYS.

BUT WHEN WE CAN READ THE RUNES ON THEM, WE SHALL KNOW MORE ABOUT THEM.

WHERE DID YOU GO TO, GANDALF, IF I MAY ASK?

I WENT TO SPY OUT OUR ROAD WHEN I MET A COUPLE OF FRIENDS OF MINE FROM RIVENDELL.

IT WAS THEY WHO TOLD ME THAT THREE TROLLS HAD COME DOWN FROM THE MOUNTAINS AND SETTLED IN THE WOODS NOT FAR FROM THE ROAD.

I IMMEDIATELY HAD A FEELING THAT I WAS WANTED BACK. PLEASE BE MORE CAREFUL, NEXT TIME, OR WE SHALL NEVER GET ANYWHERE!

THANK YOU!

They did not sing or tell stories that day, nor the next day, nor the day after. They had begun to feel that danger was not far away on either side.

IS THAT ***THE*** MOUNTAIN?

OF COURSE NOT! THAT IS ONLY THE ***BEGINNING*** OF THE MISTY MOUNTAINS—

AND IT IS A GOOD WAY EVEN FROM THE ***OTHER*** SIDE OF THEM TO THE LONELY MOUNTAIN IN THE EAST WHERE SMAUG LIES ON OUR TREASURES.

WE MUST NOT MISS THE ROAD, OR WE SHALL BE DONE FOR!

HIDDEN SOMEWHERE AHEAD OF US IS THE FAIR VALLEY OF RIVENDELL WHERE ELROND LIVES IN THE LAST HOMELY HOUSE.

I SENT A MESSAGE BY MY FRIENDS, AND WE ARE EXPECTED.

Bilbo never forgot the way they slithered and slipped in the dusk down the steep zig-zag path into the secret valley of Rivendell. The air grew warmer as they got lower...
...and their spirits rose as they went down and down.
HERE IT IS AT LAST!
HMMM! IT SMELLS LIKE ELVES!
There were elves of course. Soon Bilbo caught glimpses of them as the darkness deepened. He loved elves, though he seldom met them; but he was a little frightened of them too.
Dwarves don't get on well with elves.
Even decent enough dwarves like Thorin and his friends think them foolish (which is a very foolish thing to think), or get annoyed with them. For some elves tease them and laugh at them, and most of all at their beards.
WELCOME TO THE VALLEY!
YOU ARE A LITTLE OUT OF YOUR WAY.
WE WILL SET YOU RIGHT, BUT YOU HAD BEST GET ON FOOT, UNTIL YOU ARE OVER THE BRIDGE.
THANK YOU.
DON'T DIP YOUR BEARD IN THE FOAM, FATHER! IT IS LONG ENOUGH WITHOUT WATERING IT.
HUSH, HUSH! GOOD PEOPLE! AND GOOD NIGHT! VALLEYS HAVE EARS, AND SOME ELVES HAVE OVER MERRY TONGUES. GOOD NIGHT!
And so at last they all came to the Last Homely House, and found its doors flung wide.

Now it is a strange thing, but things that are good to have and days that are good to spend are soon told about, and not much to listen to; while things that are uncomfortable, palpitating, and even gruesome, may make a good tale, and take a deal of telling anyway.

Elrond, that master of the house, was an elf-friend. In those days of our tale there were still some people who had both elves and heroes of the North for ancestors, and Elrond was their chief.

He comes into many tales, but his part in the story of Bilbo's great adventure is only a small one, though important, as you will see, if we ever get to the end of it.

They stayed long in that good house, fourteen days at least, and they found it hard to leave.

Bilbo would gladly have stopped there for ever and ever—even supposing a wish would have taken him right back to his hobbit-hole without trouble.

So the time came to mid-summer eve, and they were to go on again with the early sun on midsummer morning.
Elrond knew all about runes of every kind. That day he looked at the swords they had brought from the troll's lair.

THESE ARE NOT TROLL-MAKE. THEY ARE OLD SWORDS, VERY OLD SWORDS OF THE HIGH ELVES OF THE WEST, MY KIN.
THEY WERE MADE IN GONDOLIN FOR THE GOBLIN-WARS.
THEY MUST HAVE COME FROM A DRAGON'S HOARD OR GOBLIN PLUNDER, FOR DRAGONS AND GOBLINS DESTROYED THAT CITY MANY AGES AGO.

THIS, THORIN, THE RUNES NAME ORCRIST, THE GOBLIN-CLEAVER IN THE ANCIENT TONGUE OF GONDOLIN; IT WAS A FAMOUS BLADE.
THIS, GANDALF, WAS GLAMDRING, FOE-HAMMER THAT THE KING OF GONDOLIN ONCE WORE.
KEEP THEM WELL!
I WILL KEEP THIS SWORD IN HONOUR. MAY IT SOON CLEAVE GOBLINS ONCE AGAIN!
A WISH THAT IS LIKELY TO BE GRANTED SOON ENOUGH IN THE MOUNTAINS! BUT SHOW ME NOW YOUR MAP!
WHAT IS THIS?
THERE ARE MOON-LETTERS HERE, BESIDE THE PLAIN RUNES WHICH SAY "FIVE FEET HIGH THE DOOR AND THREE MAY WALK ABREAST."
WHAT ARE MOON-LETTERS?

The next morning was a mid-summer's morning as fair and fresh as could be dreamed: blue sky and never a cloud, and the sun dancing on the water.

Now they rode away amid songs of farewell and good speed, with their hearts ready for more adventure, and with a knowledge of the road they must follow over the Misty Mountains to the land beyond.

There were many paths that led up into those mountains, and many passes over them. But most of the paths were cheats and deceptions and led nowhere or to bad ends; and most of the passes were infested by evil things and dreadful dangers.

The dwarves and the hobbit, helped by the wise advice of Elrond and the knowledge and memory of Gandalf, took the right road to the right pass.

Long days after they had climbed out of the valley and left the Last Homely House miles behind, they were still going up and up and up.

Far, far away in the West, Bilbo knew there lay his own country of safe and comfortable things, and his little hobbit-hole. But it was getting bitter cold up here, and the wind came shrill among the rocks.

THE SUMMER IS GETTING ON DOWN BELOW, AND HAYMAKING IS GOING ON AND PICNICS.

THEY WILL BE HARVESTING AND BLACKBERRYING, BEFORE WE EVEN **BEGIN** TO GO DOWN THE OTHER SIDE AT THIS RATE.

Gandalf only shook his head and said nothing. He knew how evil and danger had grown and thriven in the Wild, since the dragons had driven men from the lands, and the goblins had spread in secret after the battle of the Mines of Moria.

He hardly dared to hope that they would pass without fearful adventure over those great tall mountains with lonely peaks and valleys where no king ruled.
They did not.
All was well, until one day they met a thunderstorm — more than a thunderstorm, a thunder-battle.
Lightning splintered on the peaks, and rocks shivered, and great crashes split the air and rolled and tumbled into every cave and hollow; and the darkness was filled with overwhelming noise and sudden light.

Bilbo had never seen or imagined anything of the kind.
OH, DEAR!

In the lightning-flashes, he saw that across the valley the stone-giants were out.

They were hurling rocks at one another for a game, and catching them, and tossing them down into the darkness where they smashed among the trees far below, or splintered into little bits with a bang.
Then came a wind and a rain, and the wind whipped the rain and the hail about in every direction. Soon they were getting drenched and their ponies were whinnying with fright.
They could hear the giants guffawing and shouting all over the mountainsides.
THIS WON'T DO AT ALL!
IF WE DON'T GET BLOWN OFF OR DROWNED, OR STRUCK BY LIGHTNING, WE SHALL BE PICKED UP BY SOME GIANT AND KICKED SKY-HIGH FOR A FOOTBALL.

THORIN! WE HAVE FOUND A DRY CAVE NOT FAR ROUND THE NEXT CORNER; AND PONIES AND ALL COULD GET INSIDE.
HAVE YOU THOROUGHLY EXPLORED IT?
YES, YES! IT ISN'T ALL THAT BIG, AND IT DOES NOT GO FAR BACK.
GOOD ENOUGH. LET US HAVE A LOOK AT THIS CAVE, THEN.

THE FLOOR IS DRY AND IT IS OUT OF THE RAIN.
IT WILL DO— BUT NO FIRES! WE SHALL HAVE TO GET BY WITH A CHANGE INTO DRY CLOTHES.

So they spread out their wet things on the floor and then they made their blankets comfortable.

They talked and talked, and forgot about the storm, and discussed what each would do with his share of the treasure (when they got it, which at the moment did not seem so impossible).

And so they dropped off to sleep one by one.
And that was the last time that they used the ponies, packages, and paraphernalia that they had brought with them.

It turned out a good thing that night that they had brought little Bilbo with them, after all. For somehow, he could not go to sleep for a long while; and when he did sleep, he had very nasty dreams.
NEEEEEEE...
KLIK

He dreamed that a crack in the wall at the back of the cave got bigger and bigger, and opened wider and wider, and he was very afraid but could not call out or do anything but lie and look.
Then he dreamed that the floor of the cave was giving way, and he was slipping —beginning to fall down, down, goodness knows where to.
TOK CLOP!
WHA...?!
OH, DEAR! IT'S NOT A DREAM — IT'S TRUE!
A CRACK!
THIEVES!
THE PONIES!
UH?
WHUH?
HAR HAR!
GOBLINS!
HO HO, ME LADS!
GOBLINS?

Yes, goblins! There were six to each dwarf, at least, and two even for Bilbo; and they were all grabbed and carried through the crack, before you could say **tinder and flint.**

But not Gandalf.

Bilbo's yell had done that much good.

But the crack closed with a snap, and Bilbo and the dwarves were on the wrong side of it!

Now goblins are cruel, wicked, and bad-hearted. They make no beautiful things, but they make many clever ones.

Hammers, axes, swords, daggers, pickaxes, tongs, and also instruments of torture, they make very well.

SWSH

SMAK

It is not unlikely that they invented some of the machines that have since troubled the world, especially the ingenious devices for killing large numbers of people at once.

WHO ARE THESE MISERABLE PERSONS?
DWARVES, AND THIS!
WE FOUND THEM ON OUR FRONT PORCH!
UP TO NO GOOD, I'LL WARRANT! SPYING ON THE PRIVATE BUSINESS OF MY PEOPLE, I GUESS!
THIEVES, I SHOULDN'T BE SURPRISED TO LEARN!
MUR-DERERS AND FRIENDS OF ELVES, NOT UNLIKELY!
COME! WHAT HAVE YOU GOT TO SAY?

THORIN THE DWARF AT YOUR SERVICE!
WE SHELTERED FROM A STORM IN WHAT SEEMED A CONVENIENT CAVE AND UNUSED; NOTHING WAS FURTHER FROM OUR THOUGHTS THAN INCONVENIENCING GOBLINS IN ANY WAY WHATEVER.
UM! SO YOU SAY!
MIGHT I ASK WHAT YOU WERE DOING UP IN THE MOUNTAINS AT ALL, AND WHERE YOU WERE COMING FROM, AND WHERE YOU WERE GOING TO?
IN FACT I SHOULD LIKE TO KNOW ALL ABOUT YOU, THORIN OAKENSHIELD!
I KNOW TOO MUCH ABOUT YOUR FOLK ALREADY; BUT LET'S HAVE THE TRUTH, OR I WILL PREPARE SOMETHING PARTICULARLY UNCOMFORTABLE FOR YOU!
WE WERE ON A JOURNEY TO VISIT OUR RELATIVES WHO LIVE ON THE EAST SIDE OF THESE TRULY HOSPITABLE MOUNTAINS.
HE IS A LIAR, O TRULY TREMENDOUS ONE!
SEVERAL OF OUR PEOPLE WERE STRUCK BY LIGHTNING IN THE CAVE, WHEN WE INVITED THESE CREATURES TO COME BELOW; AND THEY ARE AS DEAD AS STONES.
ALSO HE HAS NOT EXPLAINED THIS!
ORCRIST! THE GOBLIN-CLEAVER! BITER!
THE THRICE CURSED SWORD OF THE ELVES OF GONDOLIN!
MURDERS AND ELF-FRIENDS!

SLASH THEM!
BEAT THEM!
BITE THEM!
GNASH THEM!
TAKE THEM AWAY AWAY TO DARK HOLES FULL OF SNAKES, AND NEVER LET THEM SEE THE LIGHT AGAIN!
FOOSH
PFFF
PFFF
PFFF
PFFF
WHAT IS THIS?
KROOOSHHHH
KROOOSHH
AAAAAA!
RUN!
YAAA!
AAAH!

OH, DEAR

SCHRANNG

GLAM-DRING!
WE ARE LOST!
WE ARE DOOMED!
THE FOE-HAMMER! BEATER!

FOLLOW ME QUICK!

QUICKER, QUICKER! THE TORCHES WILL SOON BE RELIT.

HALF A MINUTE!
MISTER BAGGINS, IT SEEMS YOU LAG BEHIND.
MY STRIDE IS NOT AS GREAT AS YOURS AND THE OTHERS.

HURRY AND CLIMB ON.

WE CANNOT LEAVE OUR BURGLAR BEHIND THIS LATE IN THE GAME.

COME, DORI. LET ME REMOVE YOUR CHAINS.

CRANNG!

THERE NOW. ARE WE ALL HERE?

LET ME SEE; ONE— THAT'S THORIN.

THANK YOU.

TWO, THREE, FOUR, FIVE, SIX, SEVEN, EIGHT, NINE, TEN, ELEVEN—

WHERE ARE FILI AND KILI?

On they went.

Gandalf was quite right: they began to hear goblin noises and horrible cries far behind in the passages they had come through. That sent them on faster than ever.
And as poor Bilbo could not possibly go half as fast as the dwarves, they took it in turn to carry him on their backs.
WHY, O WHY DID I EVER LEAVE MY HOBBIT-HOLE!
WHY, O WHY DID I EVER BRING A WRETCHED LITTLE HOBBIT ON A TREASURE HUNT!
Still goblins go faster than dwarves, and soon they could hear the flap of the goblin feet, many many feet which seemed only just round the last corner.
ABOUT TURN! DRAW YOUR SWORD, THORIN!
URK!
BITER!
BEATER!
BITER AND BEATER!
FLEE!

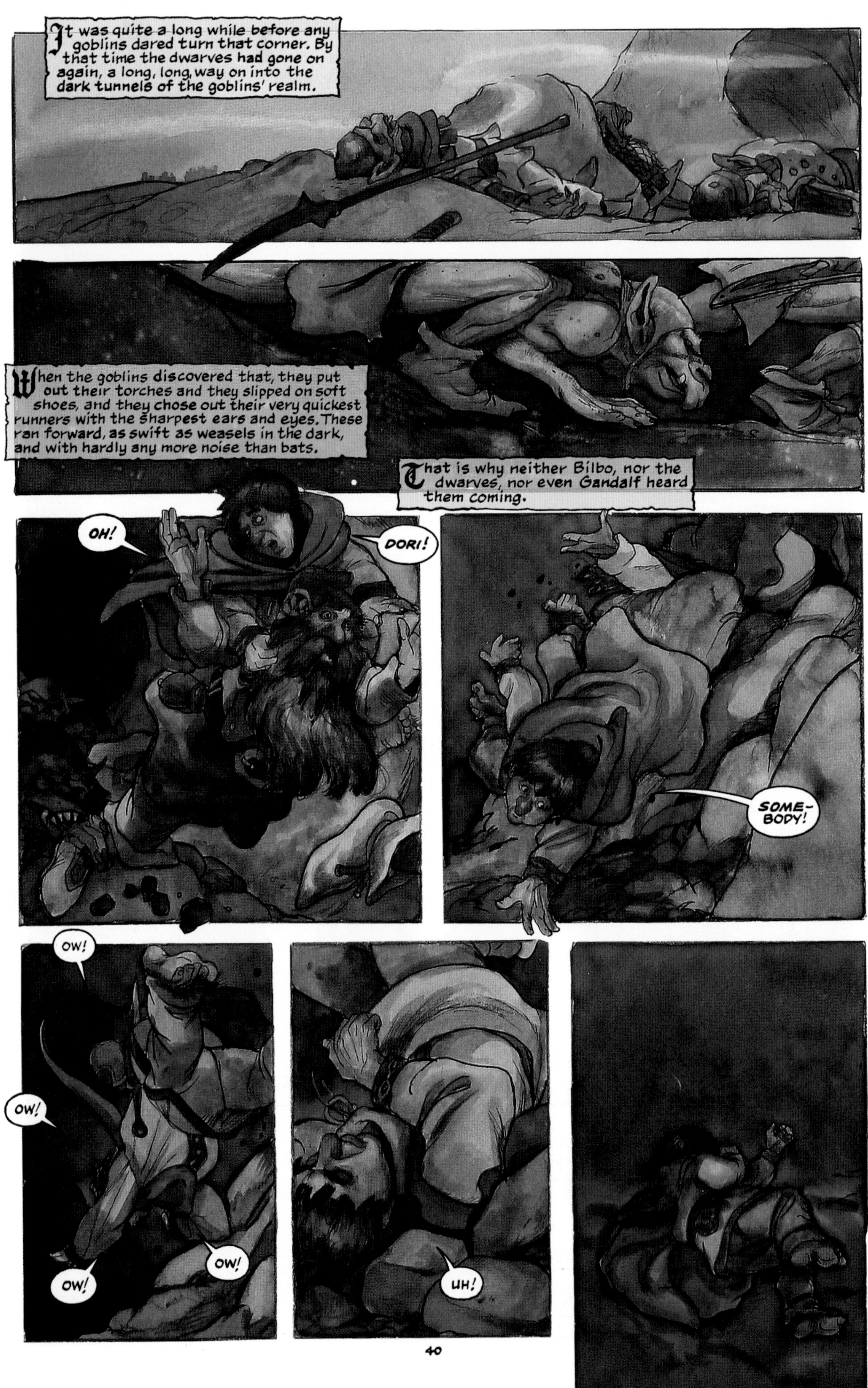
It was quite a long while before any goblins dared turn that corner. By that time the dwarves had gone on again, a long, long, way on into the dark tunnels of the goblins' realm.
When the goblins discovered that, they put out their torches and they slipped on soft shoes, and they chose out their very quickest runners with the sharpest ears and eyes. These ran forward, as swift as weasels in the dark, and with hardly any more noise than bats.
That is why neither Bilbo, nor the dwarves, nor even Gandalf heard them coming.
OH!
DORI!
SOME-BODY!
OW!
OW!
OW!
OW!
UH!

When Bilbo opened his eyes, he wondered if he had; for it was just as dark as with them shut. No one was anywhere near him. Just imagine his fright!
GANDALF?
THORIN?
DORI?
It was then that Bilbo's hand met a cold metal object in the dark.
HUH?
A RING?
NO TIME TO LOOK AT IT NOW. I'VE GOT TO FIND A WAY OUT OF THIS TERRIBLE PLACE.
It was a turning point in his career, but he did not know it.
WHERE ARE THE OTHERS?
AM I THE ONLY ONE LEFT?
AT LEAST I STILL HAVE MY PIPE.
IF ONLY I CAN FIND SOME MATCH—
HMM? WHAT'S THIS?
MY TROLL SWORD! SO IT IS AN ELVISH BLADE TOO.
AND FROM ITS GLOW I SEE GOBLINS ARE NOT VERY NEAR, AND YET NOT FAR ENOUGH.

GO BACK? NO GOOD AT ALL! GO SIDEWAYS? IMPOSSIBLE! GO FORWARD?
ONLY THING TO DO! ON WE GO!

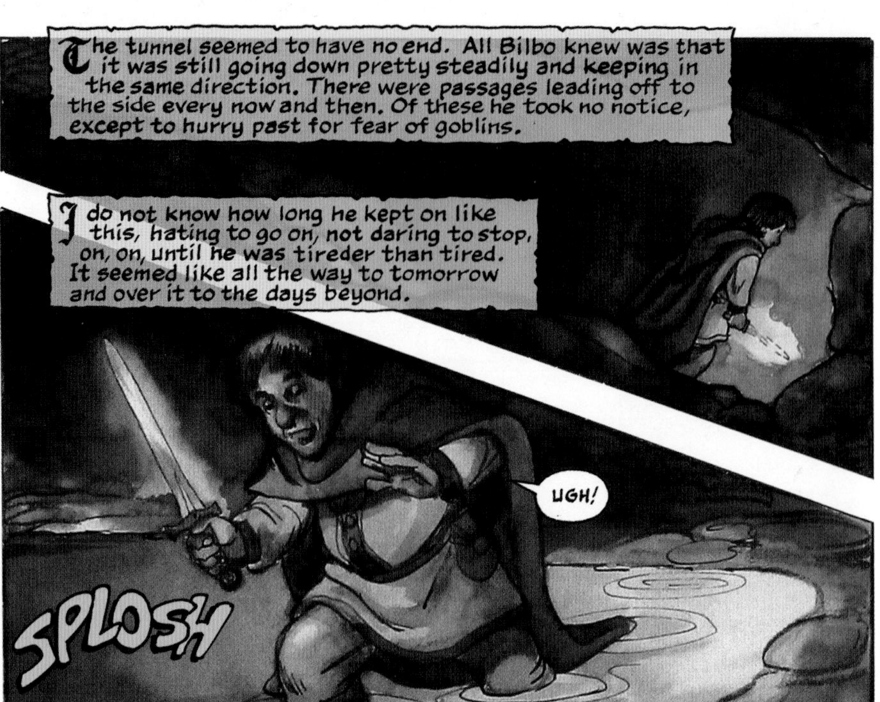
The tunnel seemed to have no end. All Bilbo knew was that it was still going down pretty steadily and keeping in the same direction. There were passages leading off to the side every now and then. Of these he took no notice, except to hurry past for fear of goblins.
I do not know how long he kept on like this, hating to go on, not daring to stop, on, on, until he was tireder than tired. It seemed like all the way to tomorrow and over it to the days beyond.
UGH!
SPLOSH

I DON'T HEAR THE SOUND OF RUNNING WATER, SO IT IS A POOL OR A LAKE, AND NOT AN UNDERGROUND RIVER I'VE FOUND. AND IT'S PROBABLY FULL OF SLIMY THINGS, WITH BIG BULGING BLIND EYES, WRIGGLING IN THE WATER.
NOW WHICH WAY DO I GO?

There are strange things living in the pools and lakes in the hearts of mountains: fish whose fathers swam in, goodness only knows how many years ago, and never swam out again; also there are other things more slimy than fish.
Even in the tunnels and caves the goblins have made for themselves there are other things living unbeknown to them that have sneaked in from outside to lie up in the dark.

Deep down here by the dark water lived old Gollum.

I don't know where he came from, nor who or what he was. He was Gollum — a name he got for the horrible swallowing noise he made in his throat, though he always called himself "my precious."
BLESS US AND SPLASH US, MY PRECIOUSSSS! I GUESS IT'S A CHOICE FEAST; AT LEAST A TASTY MORSEL IT'D MAKE US, *gollum*!
WHO ARE *YOU*?
WHAT ISS HE, MY PRECIOUSS?
I AM MISTER BILBO BAGGINS.
I HAVE LOST THE DWARVES AND I HAVE LOST THE WIZARD, AND I DON'T KNOW WHERE I AM.
AND I DON'T WANT TO KNOW, IF ONLY I CAN GET AWAY.

WHAT'S HE GOT IN HIS HANDSES ?
A SWORD, A BLADE WHICH CAME OUT OF GONDOLIN!
SSSS

PRAPS YE SITS HERE AND CHATS WITH IT A BITSY, MY PRECIOUSSS.
IT LIKES RIDDLES, PRAPS IT DOES, DOES IT?

Gollum was anxious to appear friendly, and riddles was all he could think of. Asking them had been the only game he had ever played, sitting in his hole in the long, long ago, before he crept down into the dark under the mountains.
VERY WELL.
YOU ASK FIRST.
WHAT HAS ROOTS AS NOBODY SEES, IS TALLER THAN TREES, UP, UP IT GOES AND YET NEVER GROWS?

EASY! MOUNTAIN, I SUPPOSE.
DOES IT GUESS EASY? IT MUST HAVE A COMPETITION WITH US, MY PRECIOUSS! IF IT ASKS US, AND WE DOESN'T ANSWER, THEN WE DOES WHAT IT WANTS, *eh?* WE SHOWS IT THE WAY OUT, YES!

IF PRECIOUS ASKS, AND IT DOESN'T ANSWER, WE **EATS** IT. *gollum!*

ALL RIGHT!
SSSSS
Bilbo didn't dare to disagree, and nearly burst his brain to think of riddles that could save him from being eaten.
THIRTY WHITE HORSES ON A RED HILL, FIRST THEY CHAMP, THEN THEY STAMP, THEN THEY STAND STILL.
CHESTNUTS, CHESTNUTS.
TEETH! TEETH! MY PRECIOUSSS; BUT WE HAS ONLY SIX!

VOICELESS IT CRIES,
WINGLESS FLUTTERS,
TOOTHLESS BITES,
MOUTHLESS MUTTERS.
HALF A MOMENT!

Fortunately Bilbo had once heard something rather like this before, and getting his wits back he thought of the answer.
WIND, WIND OF COURSE.

Bilbo was so pleased that he made up one on the spot. "This'll puzzle the nasty little underground creature," he thought:
AN EYE IN A BLUE FACE
SAW AN EYE IN A GREEN FACE.
"THAT EYE IS LIKE TO THIS EYE"
SAID THE FIRST EYE,
"BUT IN LOW PLACE,
NOT IN HIGH PLACE."

Gollum had been underground a long, long time, and was forgetting this sort of thing, but he brought up memories of ages and ages and ages before, when he lived with his grandmother in a hole in a bank by a river.
SS, SS, SS

SSS, SSS, MY PRECIOUSS. SUN ON THE DAISIES IT MEANS, IT DOES.

But these ordinary aboveground everyday sort of riddles were tiring for Gollum. What is more they made him hungry; so this time he tried something a bit more difficult and more unpleasant:
IT CANNOT BE SEEN, CANNOT BE FELT, CANNOT BE HEARD, CANNOT BE SMELT.
IT LIES BEHIND STARS AND UNDER HILLS, AND EMPTY HOLES IT FILLS.
IT COMES FIRST AND FOLLOWS AFTER, ENDS LIFE, KILLS LAUGHTER.

Unfortunately for Gollum, Bilbo had heard that sort of thing before; and the answer was all round him anyway.

DARK!

A BOX WITHOUT HINGES, KEY, OR LID, YET GOLDEN TREASURE INSIDE IS HID.

Bilbo asked this one to gain time, until he could think of a really hard one. Though he thought it a dreadfully easy chestnut, it proved a nasty poser for Gollum.

...KEY OR LID... SSS... GOLDEN TREASURE... INSIDE... SSSS.

WELL, WHAT IS IT? THE ANSWER'S NOT A KETTLE BOILING OVER, AS YOU SEEM TO THINK FROM THE NOISE YOU ARE MAKING.

GIVE US A CHANCE; LET IT GIVE US A CHANCE, MY PRECIOUSS— SS—SS.

WELL, WHAT ABOUT YOUR GUESS?

Suddenly Gollum remembered thieving from nests long ago, and sitting under the river bank teaching his grandmother, teaching his grandmother to suck—

EGGSES! EGGSES IT IS!

ALIVE WITHOUT BREATH, AS COLD AS DEATH; NEVER THIRSTY, EVER DRINKING, ALL IN MAIL NEVER CLINKING.

I imagine you know the answer, of course, or can guess it as easy as winking, since you are sitting comfortably at home and have not the danger of being eaten to disturb your thinking.

Bilbo sat and cleared his throat once or twice, but no answer came.

IS IT NICE, MY PRECIOUSSS? IS IT JUICY? IS IT SCRUMPTIOUSLY CRUNCHABLE?

HALF A MOMENT. I GAVE YOU A GOOD LONG CHANCE JUST NOW.

IT MUST MAKE HASTE, ***HASTE!***

SPISH

Ugh! IT IS COLD AND CLAMMY!

FISH! FISH! IT IS ***FISH!***

NO-LEGS LAY ON ONE-LEG, TWO-LEGS SAT NEAR ON THREE-LEGS, FOUR-LEGS GOT SOME.
It was not really the right time for this riddle, but Bilbo was in a hurry. Gollum might have had some trouble guessing it, if Bilbo had asked it at another time. As it was, talking of fish, "no-legs" was not so very difficult, and after that the rest was easy.
FISH ON A LITTLE TABLE, MAN AT TABLE SITTING ON A STOOL, THE CAT HAS THE BONES.
Then Gollum thought the time had come to ask something hard and horrible.
THIS THING ALL THINGS DEVOURS: BIRDS, BEASTS, TREES, FLOWERS; GNAWS IRON, BITES STEEL; GRINDS HARD STONES TO MEAL; SLAYS KING, RUINS TOWN, AND BEATS HIGH MOUNTAIN DOWN.
Poor Bilbo sat in the dark thinking of all the horrible names of all the giants and ogres he had ever heard told of in tales, but not one of them had done all these things.
He had a feeling that the answer was quite different and that he ought to know it, but he could not think of it.

Bilbo began to get frightened, and that is bad for thinking.
His tongue seemed to stick in his mouth; he wanted to shout out: "Give me more time! Give me time!" But all that came out with a sudden squeal was:
TIME! TIME!
Bilbo was saved by pure luck. For that of course was the answer.
IT'S GOT TO ASK USS A QUESTION, MY PRECIOUSS, YES, YESS, YESSS. JUSST ONE MORE QUESSTION TO GUESS, YES, YESS.
UMM...

But Bilbo simply could not think of any question with that nasty wet cold thing sitting next to him, and pawing and poking him.
ASK US! ASK US!

Bilbo pinched himself and slapped himself; he gripped on his little sword; he even felt in his pocket with his other hand. There he found the ring he had picked up in the passage and forgotten about.
WHAT HAVE I GOT IN MY POCKET ?

NOT FAIR! NOT FAIR!
IT ISN'T FAIR, MY PRECIOUS, IS IT, TO ASK US WHAT IT'S GOT IN ITS NASSTY LITTLE POCKETSES?

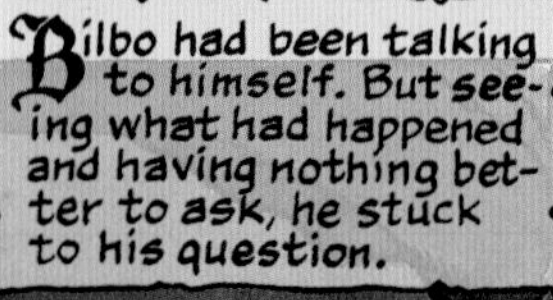
Bilbo had been talking to himself. But seeing what had happened and having nothing better to ask, he stuck to his question.

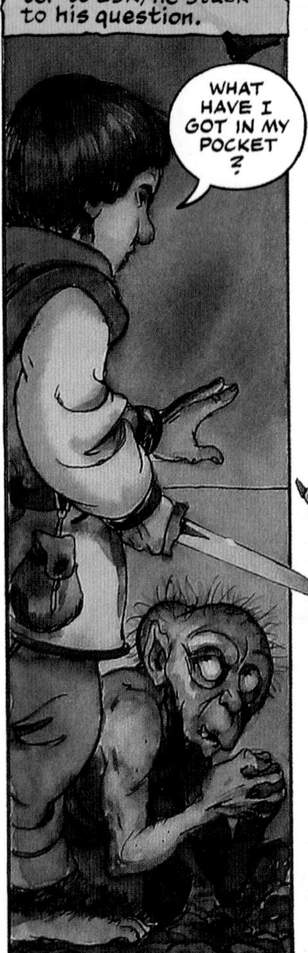
WHAT HAVE I GOT IN MY POCKET ?

S-S-S-S-S
IT MUST GIVE US THREE GUESSESES, MY PRECIOUSS, THREE GUESSESES.
VERY WELL! GUESS AWAY!
HANDSES!

WRONG. GUESS AGAIN!
S-S-S-S-S KNIFE!
WRONG! LAST GUESS!
COME ON! I AM WAITING!

TIME'S UP!
STRING, OR NOTHING!

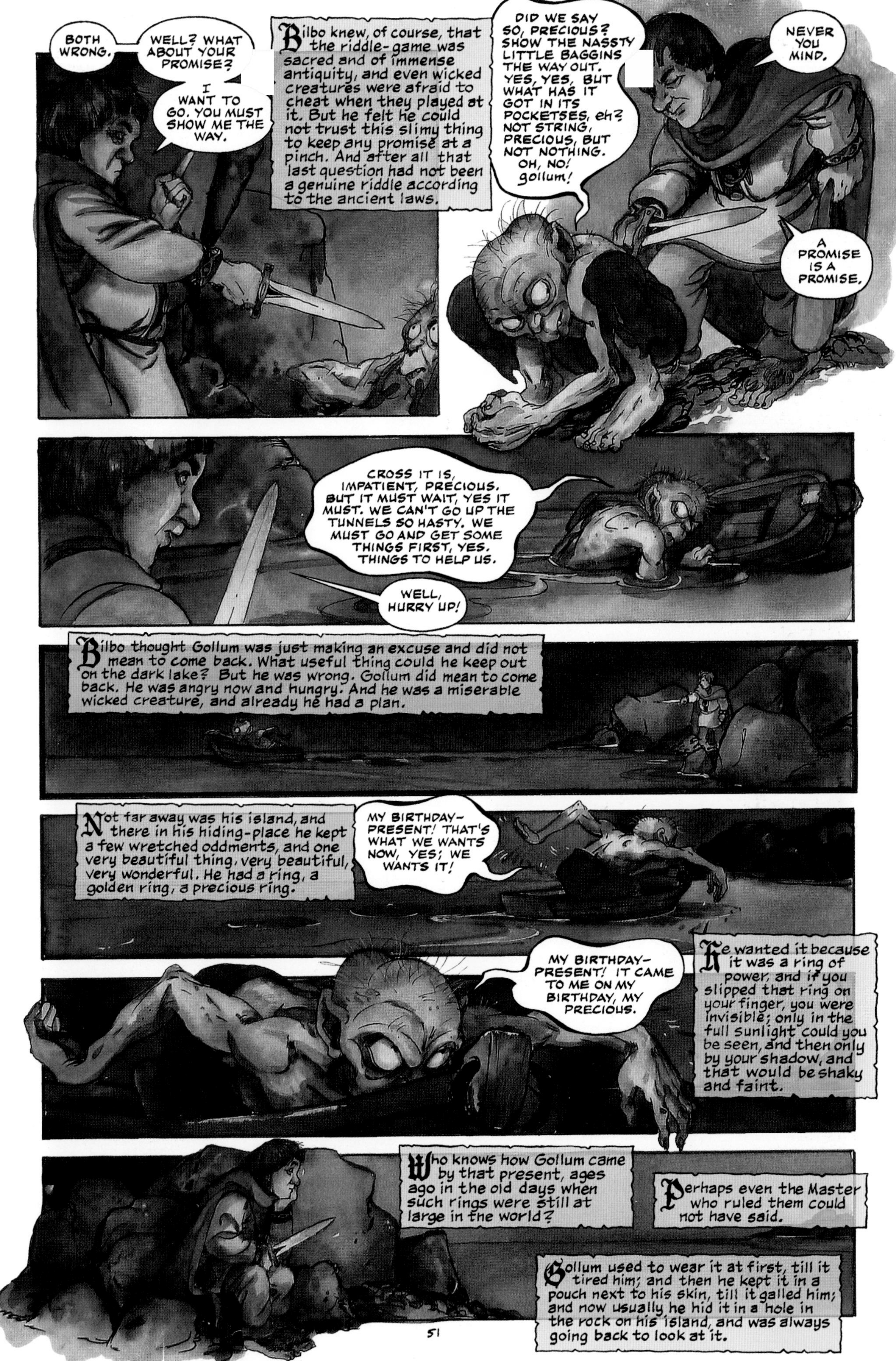
BOTH WRONG.
WELL? WHAT ABOUT YOUR PROMISE?
I WANT TO GO. YOU MUST SHOW ME THE WAY.
Bilbo knew, of course, that the riddle-game was sacred and of immense antiquity, and even wicked creatures were afraid to cheat when they played at it. But he felt he could not trust this slimy thing to keep any promise at a pinch. And after all that last question had not been a genuine riddle according to the ancient laws.
DID WE SAY SO, PRECIOUS? SHOW THE NASSTY LITTLE BAGGINS THE WAY OUT. YES, YES, BUT WHAT HAS IT GOT IN ITS POCKETSES, eh? NOT STRING, PRECIOUS, BUT NOT NOTHING. OH, NO! gollum!
NEVER YOU MIND.
A PROMISE IS A PROMISE.
CROSS IT IS, IMPATIENT, PRECIOUS. BUT IT MUST WAIT, YES IT MUST. WE CAN'T GO UP THE TUNNELS SO HASTY. WE MUST GO AND GET SOME THINGS FIRST, YES. THINGS TO HELP US.
WELL, HURRY UP!
Bilbo thought Gollum was just making an excuse and did not mean to come back. What useful thing could he keep out on the dark lake? But he was wrong. Gollum did mean to come back. He was angry now and hungry. And he was a miserable wicked creature, and already he had a plan.
Not far away was his island, and there in his hiding-place he kept a few wretched oddments, and one very beautiful thing, very beautiful, very wonderful. He had a ring, a golden ring, a precious ring.
MY BIRTHDAY-PRESENT! THAT'S WHAT WE WANTS NOW, YES; WE WANTS IT!
MY BIRTHDAY-PRESENT! IT CAME TO ME ON MY BIRTHDAY, MY PRECIOUS.
He wanted it because it was a ring of power, and if you slipped that ring on your finger, you were invisible; only in the full sunlight could you be seen, and then only by your shadow, and that would be shaky and faint.
Who knows how Gollum came by that present, ages ago in the old days when such rings were still at large in the world?
Perhaps even the Master who ruled them could not have said.
Gollum used to wear it at first, till it tired him; and then he kept it in a pouch next to his skin, till it galled him; and now usually he hid it in a hole in the rock on his island, and was always going back to look at it.

Only a few hours ago he had worn it, and caught a small goblin-imp. How it squeaked!
QUITE SAFE, YES. IT WON'T SEE US, WILL IT, MY PRECIOUS? NO. IT WON'T SEE US, AND ITS NASSTY LITTLE SWORD WILL BE USELESS, YES QUITE.

WHERE IS IT? WHERE ISS IT?

LOSST IT IS, MY PRECIOUS, LOST, LOST! CURSE US AND CRUSH US, MY PRECIOUS IS LOST!

WELL, SO AM I, AND I WANT TO GET UNLOST. AND I WON THE GAME, AND YOU PROMISED. SO COME ALONG! COME AND LET ME OUT, AND THEN GO ON WITH YOUR LOOKING!

NO, NOT YET, PRECIOUS! WE MUST SEARCH FOR IT, IT'S LOST, gollum!
BUT YOU NEVER GUESSED MY LAST QUESTION, AND YOU PROMISED.

NEVER GUESSED!
SSSSSSSS WHAT HAS IT GOT IN ITS POCKETSES?

WHAT HAVE YOU LOST? TELL ME THAT!

Bilbo could not guess what had maddened the wretched creature, but he saw that all was up, and that Gollum meant to murder him at any rate. Just in time he turned and ran blindly back up the dark passage down which he had come.
WHAT HAS IT GOT IN ITS POCKETSES?
WHAT HAVE I, I WONDER ?
Bilbo put his left hand in his pocket. The ring felt very cold as it quietly slipped on to his groping forefinger.
AAGH!
In a moment, Gollum was on him.
But before Bilbo could do anything, Gollum passed by, taking no notice of him. What could it mean?
CURSE THE BAGGINS! IT'S GONE! WHAT HAS IT GOT IN ITS POCKETSES? OH WE GUESS, WE GUESS, MY PRECIOUS. HE'S FOUND IT, YES HE MUST HAVE. MY BIRTHDAY-PRESENT.
WE LOST IT WHEN WE CAME THIS WAY LAST, WHEN WE TWISTED THAT NASSTY YOUNG SQUEAKER. THAT'S IT. CURSE IT! IT SLIPPED FROM US, AFTER ALL THESE AGES AND AGES! IT'S GONE, gollum!
IT'S NO GOOD GOING BACK THERE TO SEARCH, NO. THE BAGGINS HAS GOT IT IN ITS POCKETSES; THE NASTY, NOSER HAS FOUND IT, WE SAYS.
BUT IT DOESN'T KNOW WHAT THE PRESENT CAN DO, DOES IT? IT DOESN'T KNOW, AND IT CAN'T GO FAR. IT'S LOST ITSELF, THE NASSTY, NOSEY THING.
YES, BUT IF IT'S GOT THE PRESENT, OUR PRECIOUS PRESENT, THEN GOBLINSES WILL GET IT, gollum! THEY'LL FIND IT, THEY'LL FIND OUT WHAT IT DOES. WE SHAN'T EVER BE SAFE AGAIN, NEVER, gollum! ONE OF THE GOBLINSES WILL PUT IT ON, AND THEN NO ONE WILL SEE HIM. HE'LL BE THERE BUT NOT SEEN; AND HE'LL COME CREEPSY AND TRICKSY AND CATCH US, gollum, gollum!
IT SAID SO, YES; BUT IT'S TRICKSY. IT WON'T SAY WHAT IT'S GOT IN ITS POCKETSES. IT KNOWS. IT KNOWS A WAY IN, IT MUST KNOW A WAY OUT, YES. IT'S OFF TO THE BACK-DOOR.
THE GOBLINSES WILL CATCH IT THEN. IT CAN'T GET OUT THAT WAY, PRECIOUS.
Ssss, Ssss, gollum! GOBLINSES!

THEN LET'S STOP TALKING, PRECIOUS, AND MAKE HASTE. IF THE BAGGINS HAS GONE THAT WAY, WE MUST GO QUICK AND SEE. GO! NOT FAR NOW. MAKE HASTE! ONE LEFT, YES. ONE RIGHT, YES.

Bilbo hurried after Gollum. His head was in a whirl of hope and wonder. It seemed that the ring he had was a magic ring: it made you invisible!

He had heard of such things, of course, in old tales; but it was hard to believe that he really had found one, by accident. Still there it was: Gollum with his bright eyes had passed him by, only a yard to one side.

As Gollum's count of side-passages grew he slowed down, and he began to get shaky and weepy; for he was leaving the water further and further behind, and he was getting afraid.

THIS IS IT. THIS IS THE WAY TO THE BACK-DOOR, YES. HERE'S THE PASSAGE!

BUT WE DURSTN'T GO IN, PRECIOUS, NO WE DURSTN'T. GOBLINSES DOWN THERE. LOTS OF GOBLINSES. WE SMELL THEM. SSSS!

WHAT SHALL WE DO? CURSE THEM AND CRUSH THEM!

WE MUST WAIT HERE, PRECIOUS, WAIT A BIT AND SEE.

So they came to a dead stop. Gollum had brought Bilbo to the way out after all, but Bilbo could not get in! Bilbo crept away from the wall more quietly than a mouse; but Gollum stiffened at once, and sniffed, and his eyes went green!

Bilbo almost stopped breathing, and went stiff himself. He was desperate. He must get away while he had any strength left. He must fight. He must stab the foul thing, put its eyes out, kill it. It meant to kill him.

No, not a fair fight. He was invisible now. Gollum had no sword. Gollum had not actually threatened to kill him, or tried to yet. And he was miserable, alone, lost.

A sudden understanding, a pity mixed with horror, welled up in Bilbo's heart: a glimpse of endless unmarked days without light or hope of betterment. And then quite suddenly, as if lifted by a new strength and resolve, he leaped.

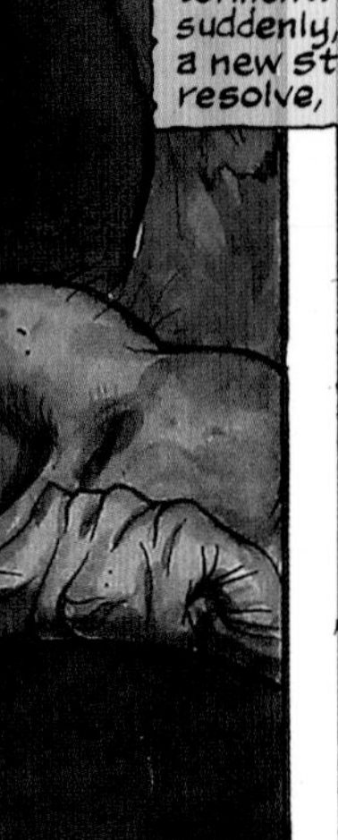

EEEEEEE!

Straight over Gollum's head he leaped, seven feet forward and three in the air.

IF GOBLINS ARE SO NEAR THAT HE SMELT THEM, THEN THEY'LL HAVE HEARD HIS SHRIEKING AND CURSING. CAREFUL NOW, OR THIS WAY WILL LEAD YOU TO WORSE THINGS.

Soon he saw, filtering round another corner—a glimpse of light. Not red light, as of fire or lantern, but a pale out-of-doors sort of light.

Then Bilbo began to run.

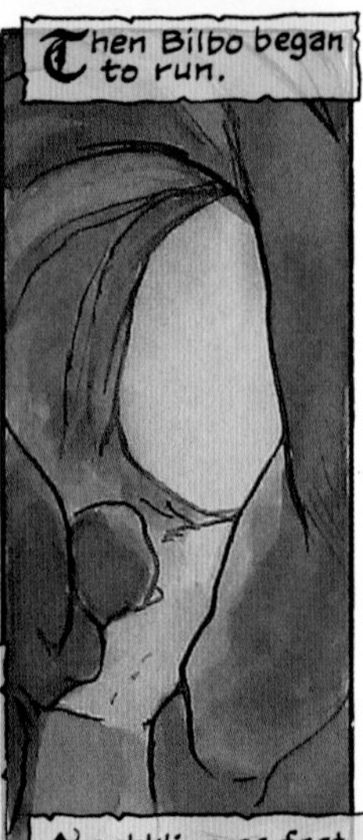

Scuttling as fast as his legs would carry him he turned the last corner...

...and came suddenly right into an open space, where the light, after all that time in the dark, seemed dazzlingly bright.
Huh?
The goblins saw Bilbo sooner than he saw them. Yes, they saw him. Whether it was an accident, or a last trick of the ring before it took a new master, it was not on his finger.
Arr! HERE'S ONE OF THEM!
HAR! HAR!
Forgetting even to draw his sword Bilbo struck his hands into his pockets. And there was the ring still, in his left pocket, and it slipped on his forefinger.
WHERE IS IT?
GO BACK UP THE PASSAGE.
THIS WAY!
THAT WAY!
Bilbo was dreadfully frightened, but he had the sense to understand what had happened and to get out of the way.
LOOK OUT FOR THE DOOR!
WHERE'S IT GONE?
The poor little hobbit dodged this way and that, was knocked over by a goblin, scrambled away on all fours just in time, got up, and ran for the door.
The door was still ajar, but a goblin had pushed it nearly to. Bilbo struggled but he could not move it. He tried to squeeze through the crack. He squeezed and squeezed, and he stuck! His buttons had got wedged on the edge of the door. He could see outside into the open air—but he could not get through.
THERE IS A SHADOW BY THE DOOR. SOMETHING IS OUTSIDE!
Bilbo was through, with a torn coat and waistcoat, leaping down the steps like a goat. Of course the goblins soon came down after him, hooting and hallooing. But they don't like the sun: it makes their legs wobble and their heads giddy. They could not find Bilbo with the ring on; so soon they went back grumbling and cursing to guard the door.
Bilbo had escaped.

GOOD HEAVENS!
I SEEM TO HAVE GOT RIGHT TO THE OTHER SIDE OF THE MISTY MOUNTAINS, RIGHT TO THE EDGE OF THE LAND BEYOND!
WHERE AND O WHERE CAN GANDALF AND THE DWARVES HAVE GOT TO? I ONLY HOPE TO GOODNESS THEY ARE NOT STILL BACK THERE IN THE POWER OF THE GOBLINS!
Bilbo wandered on, out of the little high valley, over its edge, and down the slopes beyond; but all the while a very uncomfortable thought was growing inside him.
He wondered whether he ought not, now he had the magic ring, to go back into the horrible, horrible, tunnels and look for his friends.
He had just made up his mind that it was his duty that he must turn back—and very miserable he felt about it—when he heard-
VOICES?
IT'S BALIN. AND HE DOESN'T SEE ME.
THE RING! OF COURSE HE DOESN'T SEE ME!
I WILL GIVE THEM ALL A SURPRISE.
AFTER ALL HE IS MY FRIEND, AND NOT A BAD LITTLE CHAP. I FEEL RESPONSIBLE FOR HIM. I WISH TO GOODNESS YOU HAD NOT LOST HIM.
HE HAS BEEN MORE TROUBLE THAN USE SO FAR. IF WE HAVE GOT TO GO BACK NOW INTO THOSE ABOMINABLE TUNNELS TO LOOK FOR HIM, THEN DRAT HIM, I SAY.
I BROUGHT HIM, AND I DON'T BRING THINGS THAT ARE OF NO USE. EITHER YOU HELP ME TO LOOK FOR HIM, OR I GO AND LEAVE YOU HERE TO GET OUT OF THE MESS AS BEST YOU CAN YOURSELVES.
WHATEVER DID YOU WANT TO GO AND DROP HIM FOR, DORI?
YOU WOULD HAVE DROPPED HIM IF A GOBLIN HAD SUDDENLY GRABBED YOUR LEG FROM BEHIND IN THE DARK!
THEN WHY DIDN'T YOU PICK HIM UP AGAIN?
GOOD HEAVENS! CAN YOU ASK? GOBLINS FIGHTING AND BITING IN THE DARK, EVERYBODY FALLING OVER BODIES AND HITTING ONE ANOTHER!
YOU SHOUTED 'FOLLOW ME EVERYBODY!' AND EVERYBODY OUGHT TO HAVE FOLLOWED. AND HERE WE ARE — WITHOUT THE BURGLAR, CONFUSTICATE HIM!

AND HERE'S THE BURGLAR!

Bless me, how they jumped! Then they shouted with surprise and delight.

THE BURGLAR!

BILBO!

They wanted to know all about his adventures after they had lost him, and Bilbo told them everything—except about the finding of the ring ("not just now" he thought).

...SO I JUMPED OVER GOLLUM AND ESCAPED, AND RAN DOWN TO THE GATE.
WHAT ABOUT GUARDS? WEREN'T THERE ANY?
O YES! LOTS OF THEM.
BUT I DODGED 'EM. I GOT STUCK IN THE DOOR, AND I LOST LOTS OF BUTTONS, BUT I SQUEEZED THROUGH ALL RIGHT—AND HERE I AM.

It is a fact that Bilbo's reputation went up a very great deal with the dwarves after this.
But Gandalf gave Bilbo a queer look, and the hobbit wondered if he guessed at the part of his tale that he had left out.

Then Gandalf explained how he had turned up again: how in the flash which killed the goblins that were grabbing him he had nipped inside the crack; how he followed after the drivers and prisoners right to the edge of the great hall, and there worked up the best magic he could in the shadows; and how he knew all about the backdoor, where Bilbo lost his buttons.
THEY WILL GUARD IT DOUBLY AFTER THIS.

WE MUST BE GETTING ON AT ONCE. THE GOBLINS WILL BE OUT AFTER US IN HUNDREDS WHEN NIGHT COMES ON. THEY CAN SMELL OUR FOOTSTEPS FOR HOURS AND HOURS AFTER WE HAVE PASSED. WE MUST BE MILES ON BEFORE DUSK.
O YES! YOU LOSE TRACK OF TIME INSIDE GOBLIN TUNNELS. TODAY'S THURSDAY, AND IT WAS MONDAY NIGHT OR TUESDAY MORNING THAT WE WERE CAPTURED. WE ARE TOO FAR TO THE NORTH, AND HAVE SOME AWKWARD COUNTRY AHEAD. LET'S GET ON!

As they went on the shadows deepened about them. Still they marched along as fast as they were able; and all the while the forest-gloom got heavier and the forest-silence deeper.

There was no wind that evening to bring even a sea-sighing into the branches of the trees.

MUST WE GO ANY FURTHER? MY TOES ARE ALL BRUISED AND BENT, AND MY LEGS ACHE, AND MY **STOMACH** IS WAGGING LIKE AN EMPTY SACK.

A BIT FURTHER.

AARROOoooo

WOLVES!

ROO ROO ARROOoo

WHAT SHALL WE DO, WHAT SHALL WE DO!

ESCAPING GOBLINS TO BE CAUGHT BY WOLVES!

UP THE TREES **QUICK!**

In a minute there was a whole pack of wild Wargs (for so the evil wolves over the Edge of the Wild were named) yelping all around the tree and leaping up at the trunk, with eyes blazing and tongues hanging out. They spoke in the dreadful language of the Wargs. Though Bilbo did not understand it, Gandalf did, and I will tell you what he heard.
It seemed that a great goblin raid had been planned for that very night against the bold men from the South who had been making their way into that far land, cutting down trees, and building themselves places to live. The Wargs had come to meet the goblins and the goblins were late.
The reason, no doubt, was the death of the Great Goblin, and all the excitement caused by the dwarves and Bilbo, and the wizard, for whom they were probably still hunting.
The Wargs were angry and puzzled at finding Gandalf and his friends here in their very meeting-place. They thought they were friends of the woodmen, and were come to spy on them, and would take news of their plans down into the valleys. So the Wargs had no intention of going away and letting the people up the trees escape, at any rate not until morning.
And long before that, goblin soldiers would be coming down from the mountains; and goblins can climb trees, or cut them down.
FFFT
Now you can understand why Gandalf, listening to their growling and yelping, began to be dreadfully afraid, wizard though he was. All the same he was not going to let them have it all their own way.
FUSSH
FRROOM
RAR
WHAT'S ALL THIS UPROAR IN THE FOREST TONIGHT?
I HEAR WOLVES' VOICES!
ARE THE GOBLINS AT MISCHIEF IN THE WOODS?
The lord of the eagles of the Misty Mountains had eyes that could look at the sun unblinking, and could see a rabbit moving on the ground a mile below even in the moonlight.
So though he could not see the people in the trees, he could make out the commotion among the wolves and see tiny flashes of fire.
Tonight he was filled with curiosity to know what was afoot; so he summoned many other eagles to him, and slowly they circled down, down, down.

Maddened and angry the Wargs were leaping and howling round the trees. Then suddenly goblins came running up yelling.
SLASH THEM!
BEAT THEM!
They thought a battle with the woodmen was going on; but they soon learned what had really happened. Goblins are not afraid of fire, and they soon had a plan which seemed to them most amusing.
They rushed round and stamped and beat, and beat and stamped, until nearly all the flames were put out – but they did not put out the fire nearer to the trees where the dwarves were. That fire they fed with leaves and dead branches and bracken.
FLY AWAY, LITTLE BIRDS! FLY AWAY IF YOU CAN!
FIFTEEN BIRDS IN FIVE FIRTREES, THEIR FEATHERS WERE FANNED IN A FIERY BREEZE!
SING, SING LITTLE BIRDS! WHY DON'T YOU SING?
GO AWAY! LITTLE BOYS!
IT ISN'T BIRD-NESTING TIME. ALSO NAUGHTY LITTLE BOYS THAT PLAY WITH FIRE GET PUNISHED.
BURN, BURN TREE AND FERN! SHRIVEL AND SCORCH! A FIZZLING TORCH TO LIGHT THE NIGHT FOR OUR DELIGHT, YA HEY!
And with that *Ya hey!* the flames were under Gandalf's tree. In a moment it spread to the others. The bark caught fire, the lower branches cracked.
KA-KA-ZZZAAAZZ
Then Gandalf climbed to the top of his tree. The sudden splendour flashed from his wand like lightning, as he got ready to spring down from on high right among the spears of the goblins.
But he never leaped.

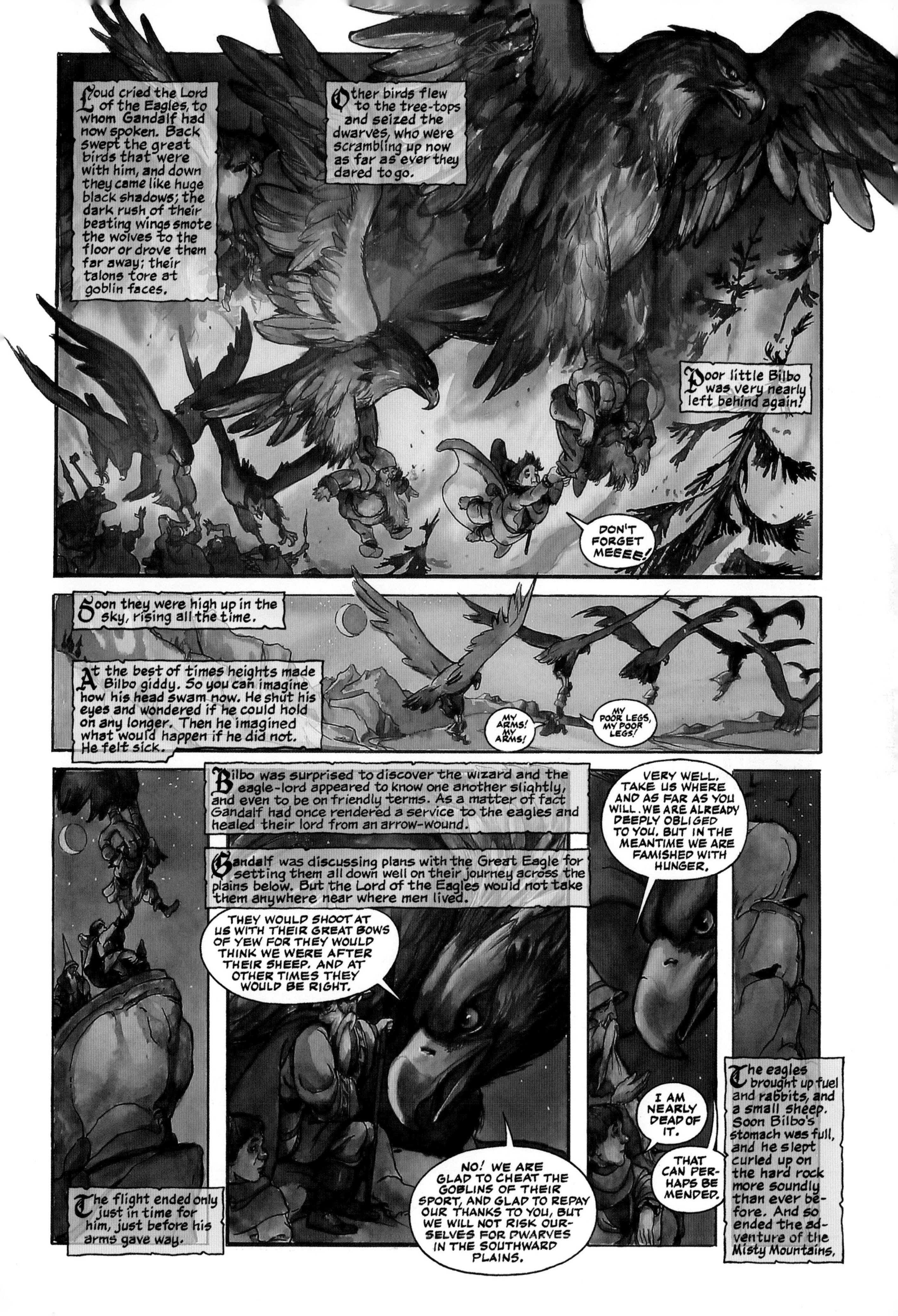

Loud cried the Lord of the Eagles, to whom Gandalf had now spoken. Back swept the great birds that were with him, and down they came like huge black shadows; the dark rush of their beating wings smote the wolves to the floor or drove them far away; their talons tore at goblin faces.

Other birds flew to the tree-tops and seized the dwarves, who were scrambling up now as far as ever they dared to go.

Poor little Bilbo was very nearly left behind again!

DON'T FORGET MEEEE!

Soon they were high up in the sky, rising all the time.

At the best of times heights made Bilbo giddy. So you can imagine how his head swam now. He shut his eyes and wondered if he could hold on any longer. Then he imagined what would happen if he did not. He felt sick.

MY ARMS! MY ARMS!

MY POOR LEGS, MY POOR LEGS!

Bilbo was surprised to discover the wizard and the eagle-lord appeared to know one another slightly, and even to be on friendly terms. As a matter of fact Gandalf had once rendered a service to the eagles and healed their lord from an arrow-wound.

Gandalf was discussing plans with the Great Eagle for setting them all down well on their journey across the plains below. But the Lord of the Eagles would not take them anywhere near where men lived.

The flight ended only just in time for him, just before his arms gave way.
THEY WOULD SHOOT AT US WITH THEIR GREAT BOWS OF YEW FOR THEY WOULD THINK WE WERE AFTER THEIR SHEEP. AND AT OTHER TIMES THEY WOULD BE RIGHT.
NO! WE ARE GLAD TO CHEAT THE GOBLINS OF THEIR SPORT, AND GLAD TO REPAY OUR THANKS TO YOU, BUT WE WILL NOT RISK OURSELVES FOR DWARVES IN THE SOUTHWARD PLAINS.

VERY WELL. TAKE US WHERE AND AS FAR AS YOU WILL. WE ARE ALREADY DEEPLY OBLIGED TO YOU. BUT IN THE MEANTIME WE ARE FAMISHED WITH HUNGER.
I AM NEARLY DEAD OF IT.
THAT CAN PERHAPS BE MENDED.

The eagles brought up fuel and rabbits, and a small sheep. Soon Bilbo's stomach was full, and he slept curled up on the hard rock more soundly than ever before. And so ended the adventure of the Misty Mountains.

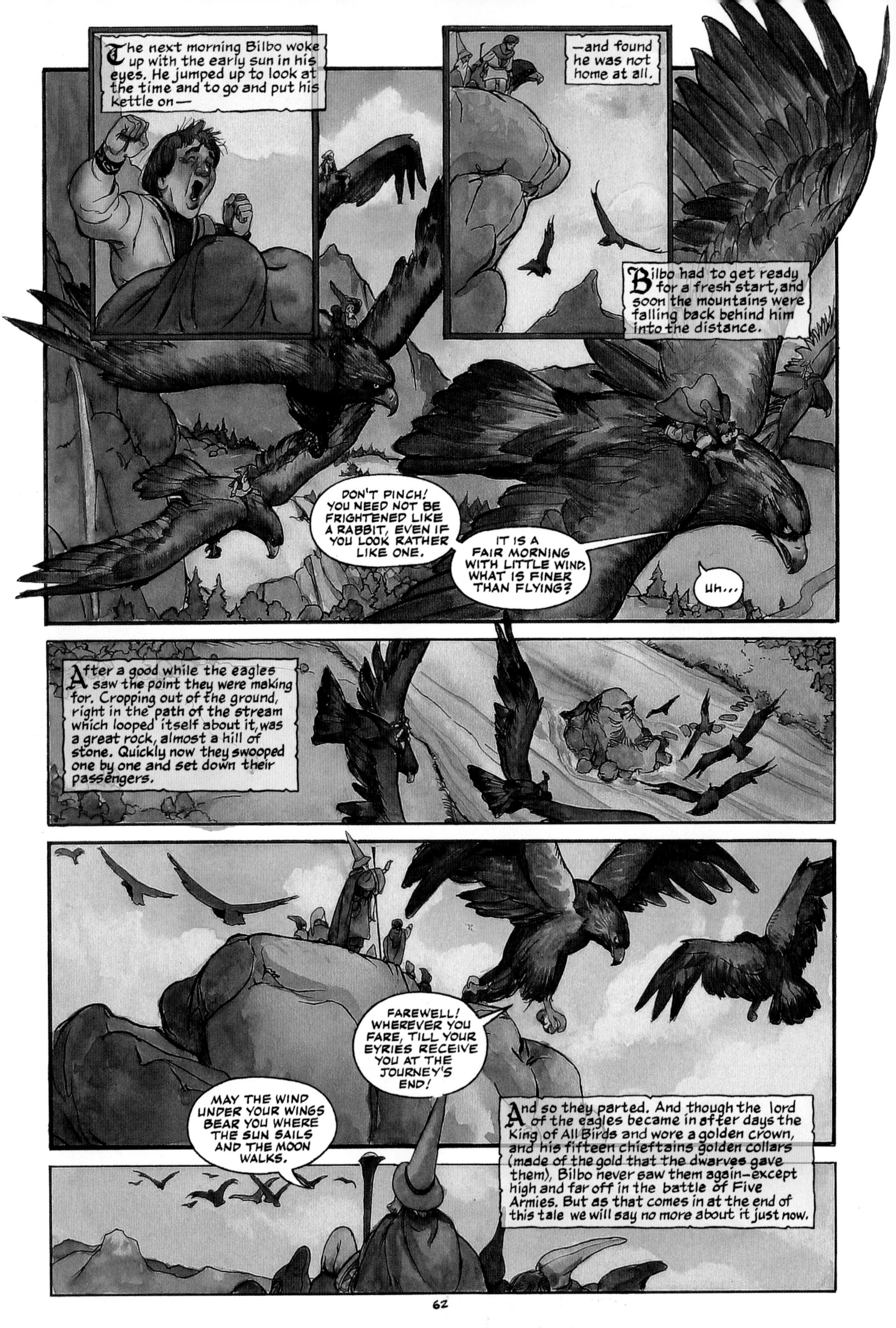

The next morning Bilbo woke up with the early sun in his eyes. He jumped up to look at the time and to go and put his kettle on—

—and found he was not home at all.

Bilbo had to get ready for a fresh start, and soon the mountains were falling back behind him into the distance.

DON'T PINCH! YOU NEED NOT BE FRIGHTENED LIKE A RABBIT, EVEN IF YOU LOOK RATHER LIKE ONE.

IT IS A FAIR MORNING WITH LITTLE WIND. WHAT IS FINER THAN FLYING?

Uh...

After a good while the eagles saw the point they were making for. Cropping out of the ground, right in the path of the stream which looped itself about it, was a great rock, almost a hill of stone. Quickly now they swooped one by one and set down their passengers.

FAREWELL! WHEREVER YOU FARE, TILL YOUR EYRIES RECEIVE YOU AT THE JOURNEY'S END!
MAY THE WIND UNDER YOUR WINGS BEAR YOU WHERE THE SUN SAILS AND THE MOON WALKS.
And so they parted. And though the lord of the eagles became in after days the King of All Birds and wore a golden crown, and his fifteen chieftains golden collars (made of the gold that the dwarves gave them), Bilbo never saw them again—except high and far off in the battle of Five Armies. But as that comes in at the end of this tale we will say no more about it just now.

I ALWAYS MEANT TO SEE YOU ALL SAFE, IF POSSIBLE, OVER THE MOUNTAINS, AND NOW BY GOOD MANAGEMENT AND GOOD LUCK I HAVE DONE IT.
INDEED WE ARE NOW A GOOD DEAL FURTHER EAST THAN I EVER MEANT TO COME WITH YOU, FOR AFTER ALL THIS IS NOT MY ADVENTURE.
I MAY LOOK IN ON IT AGAIN BEFORE IT IS ALL OVER, BUT IN THE MEANWHILE I HAVE SOME OTHER PRESSING BUSINESS TO ATTEND TO.
BUT WE THOUGHT YOU WERE GOING TO COME ALL THE WAY WITH US.
I AM NOT GOING TO DISAPPEAR THIS VERY INSTANT. PROBABLY I CAN HELP YOU OUT OF YOUR PRESENT PLIGHT, AND I NEED A LITTLE HELP MYSELF.
WE HAVE NO FOOD, AND NO BAGGAGE, AND NO PONIES TO RIDE. BUT THERE IS SOMEBODY I KNOW OF, WHO LIVES NOT FAR AWAY. WE MUST GO AND FIND HIM; AND IF ALL GOES WELL AT OUR MEETING, I THINK I SHALL BE OFF!
WHO IS THAT SOMEBODY?
A VERY GREAT PERSON. HE MADE THE STEPS ON THE GREAT ROCK—THE CARROCK I BELIEVE HE CALLS IT. HE CALLS THINGS LIKE THAT CARROCKS, AND THIS ONE IS THE CARROCK BECAUSE IT IS THE ONLY ONE NEAR HIS HOME AND HE KNOWS IT WELL.
YOU MUST ALL BE VERY POLITE WHEN I INTRODUCE YOU. HE CAN BE APPALLING WHEN HE IS ANGRY, THOUGH HE IS KIND ENOUGH IF HUMORED. STILL I WARN YOU HE GETS ANGRY EASILY.
IF YOU MUST KNOW MORE, HIS NAME IS BEORN. HE IS VERY STRONG, AND HE IS A SKIN-CHANGER.
WHAT! A FURRIER, A MAN THAT CALLS RABBITS CONIES, WHEN HE DOESN'T TURN THEIR SKINS INTO SQUIRRELS?
GOOD GRACIOUS HEAVENS, NO, NO, NO, NO! DON'T BE A FOOL MISTER BAGGINS IF YOU CAN HELP IT! HE CHANGES HIS SKIN; SOMETIMES HE IS A HUGE BLACK BEAR, SOMETIMES HE IS A GREAT STRONG BLACK-HAIRED MAN WITH HUGE ARMS AND A GREAT BEARD.
AS A MAN HE KEEPS CATTLE AND HORSES AND HIVES AND HIVES OF GREAT FIERCE BEES, AND LIVES MOST ON CREAM AND HONEY. AS A BEAR HE RANGES FAR AND WIDE.
I CANNOT TELL YOU MUCH MORE, THOUGH THAT OUGHT TO BE ENOUGH. HE IS NOT THE SORT OF PERSON TO ASK QUESTIONS OF. AT ANY RATE HE IS UNDER NO ENCHANTMENT BUT HIS OWN.
THESE BEES ARE SO BIG, IF ONE WAS TO STING ME I SHOULD SWELL UP AS BIG AGAIN AS I AM!
WE ARE GETTING NEAR. WE ARE ON THE EDGE OF HIS BEE PASTURES.

YOU HAD BETTER WAIT HERE, AND WHEN I CALL OR WHISTLE BEGIN TO COME AFTER ME—YOU WILL SEE THE WAY I GO—BUT ONLY IN SMALL GROUPS, MIND, ABOUT FIVE MINUTES APART.
COME ON MISTER BAGGINS! THERE IS A GATE SOMEWHERE ROUND THIS WAY.
THEY HAVE GONE TO TELL HIM OF THE ARRIVAL OF STRANGERS.
Ugh! HERE THEY ARE! THEY DON'T LOOK DANGEROUS.
WHO ARE YOU AND WHAT DO YOU WANT?
I AM GANDALF. THIS IS MISTER BAGGINS, A HOBBIT OF GOOD FAMILY AND UNIMPEACHABLE REPUTATION. I AM A WIZARD.
I HAVE HEARD OF YOU, IF YOU HAVE NOT HEARD OF ME; BUT PERHAPS YOU HAVE HEARD OF MY GOOD COUSIN RADAGAST WHO LIVES NEAR THE SOUTHERN BORDERS OF MIRKWOOD?
YES; NOT A BAD FELLOW AS WIZARDS GO, I BELIEVE. I USED TO SEE HIM NOW AND AGAIN.
WELL, NOW I KNOW WHO YOU ARE, OR WHO YOU **SAY** YOU ARE. WHAT DO YOU WANT?

TO TELL YOU THE TRUTH, WE HAVE LOST OUR LUGGAGE AND NEARLY LOST OUR WAY, AND ARE RATHER IN NEED OF HELP. I MAY SAY WE HAVE HAD RATHER A BAD TIME WITH GOBLINS IN THE MOUNTAINS.
GOBLINS? WHAT DID YOU GO NEAR THEM FOR?
WE DID NOT MEAN TO. WE WERE COMING— IT IS A LONG TALE.
THEN YOU HAD BETTER COME INSIDE AND TELL ME ABOUT IT, IF IT WON'T TAKE ALL DAY.

WE WERE COMING OVER THE MOUNTAINS AND TOOK REFUGE IN A CAVE. AS SOON AS WE WERE ASLEEP, GOBLINS APPEARED AND GRABBED THE HOBBIT AND OUR TROOP OF PONIES—
TROOP OF PONIES? WHAT WERE YOU— A TRAVELLING CIRCUS? OR DO YOU ALWAYS CALL TWO A TROOP?
OH NO! THERE WERE MORE THAN TWO PONIES, FOR THERE WERE MORE THAN TWO OF US. I DID NOT LIKE TO BOTHER YOU WITH A LOT OF US, UNTIL I FOUND OUT IF YOU WERE BUSY. I WILL GIVE YOU A CALL, IF I MAY.

GO ON, CALL AWAY!
WHEEET

WHERE WAS I? O YES— I WAS NOT GRABBED! I KILLED A GOBLIN OR TWO WITH A FLASH AND FOLLOWED DOWN INTO THE MAIN HALL. I THOUGHT TO MYSELF, WHAT CAN A DOZEN DO AGAINST SO MANY?
OH, HERE ARE THE OTHERS NOW.
THESE ARE NOT HOBBITS BUT DWARVES, AND THIS IS THE FIRST TIME I'VE HEARD EIGHT CALLED A DOZEN!

THEY DON'T SEEM ALL TO HAVE COME.
WHEEEEET

So Gandalf went on with the tale; how Mister Baggins had been mislaid, and the hobbit's reappearance...
...their scramble in the woods and their climbing into the trees with goblins below yelling "Fifteen birds in five fir-trees..."

GOOD HEAVENS! DON'T PRETEND THAT GOBLINS CAN'T COUNT. THEY CAN. TWELVE ISN'T FIFTEEN AND THEY KNOW IT.
AND SO DO I.

THERE WERE BIFUR AND BOFUR AS WELL. I HAVEN'T VENTURED TO INTRODUCE THEM BEFORE, AND HERE THEY ARE.
AND ME!
WELL, NOW THERE ARE FIFTEEN OF YOU; AND SINCE GOBLINS CAN COUNT, NOW PERHAPS WE CAN FINISH THIS STORY WITHOUT ANY MORE INTERRUPTIONS.
Mister Baggins saw then how clever Gandalf had been. The interruptions had really made Beorn more interested in the story, and the story had kept him from sending the dwarves off at once like suspicious beggars.
By the time the wizard had finished his tale the sun had fallen behind the peaks of the Misty Mountains and Beorn had invited them to supper.

It was a supper, or a dinner, such as they had not had since they left the Last Homely House in the West and said good-bye to Elrond.
All the time they ate, Beorn told tales of the wild lands on this side of the mountains, and especially of the terrible forest of Mirkwood.

When dinner was over the dwarves began to tell tales of their own, of gold and silver and smith-craft, but Beorn paid little heed to them— he did not appear to care for such things.
The dark night came on outside. Soon Bilbo began to nod with sleep.

IT IS TIME FOR US TO SLEEP, BUT NOT I THINK FOR BEORN.

IN THIS HALL WE CAN REST SOUND AND SAFE, BUT I WARN YOU ALL NOT TO FORGET WHAT BEORN SAID BEFORE HE LEFT US: YOU MUST NOT STRAY OUTSIDE UNTIL THE SUN IS UP, ON YOUR PERIL.

Bilbo woke in the night and heard a growling sound outside and wondered whether it could be Beorn in enchanted shape, and if he would come in as a bear and kill them. He dived under the blankets and hid his head, and fell asleep at last in spite of his fears.

It was full morning when he awoke to find there was no sign of Beorn or Gandalf. It was just before sunset when the wizard walked into the hall.

WHERE IS OUR HOST, AND WHERE HAVE ***YOU*** BEEN ALL DAY YOURSELF?

I WILL ANSWER THE SECOND QUESTION FIRST— BUT BLESS ME! THIS IS A SPLENDID PLACE FOR SMOKE-RINGS!

Indeed for a long time they could get nothing more out of him.

I HAVE BEEN PICKING OUT BEAR-TRACKS. THERE MUST HAVE BEEN A REGULAR BEARS' MEETING OUTSIDE HERE LAST NIGHT. I SOON SAW THAT BEORN COULD NOT HAVE MADE THEM ALL. THERE WERE FAR TOO MANY OF THEM, AND THEY WERE OF VARIOUS SIZES TOO. THEY CAME FROM ALMOST EVERY DIRECTION, EXCEPT FROM THE MOUNTAINS. IN THAT DIRECTION ONLY ONE SET OF FOOTPRINTS LED.
I FOLLOWED THOSE AS FAR AS I COULD. THEY WENT STRAIGHT OFF IN THE DIRECTION OF THE PINE-WOODS, WHERE WE HAD OUR PLEASANT LITTLE PARTY WITH THE WARGS THE NIGHT BEFORE LAST.
AND NOW I THINK I HAVE ANSWERED YOUR FIRST QUESTION, TOO.

WHAT SHALL WE DO IF HE LEADS ALL THE WARGS AND GOBLINS DOWN HERE? WE SHALL ALL BE CAUGHT AND KILLED!
DON'T BE SILLY! YOU HAD BETTER GO TO BED, YOUR WITS ARE SLEEPY.
The hobbit felt quite crushed, and as there seemed nothing else to do he did go to bed; and while the dwarves were still singing songs he dropped asleep. Then he woke up when everyone else was asleep, and he heard the same scraping, scuffling, snuffling, and growling as before.
SO HERE YOU ALL ARE STILL! NOT EATEN UP BY WARGS OR GOBLINS OR WICKED BEARS YET, I SEE. LITTLE BUNNY IS GETTING NICE AND FAT AGAIN ON BREAD AND HONEY. COME AND HAVE SOME MORE.
So they all went to breakfast with him. He set them laughing with his funny stories, then told them where he had been and why.
He had been over the river and right up into the mountains. From the burnt wolf-glade he had soon found out that part of their story was true; then he caught a Warg and a goblin wandering in the woods. From these he had got news: the goblin patrols were still hunting with Wargs for the dwarves, the Great Goblin was dead, and a raid might soon be made to find the dwarves.
IT WAS A GOOD STORY, THAT OF YOURS, BUT I LIKE IT STILL BETTER NOW I AM SURE IT IS TRUE. AS IT IS, I HAVE HURRIED HOME AS FAST AS I COULD TO SEE THAT YOU WERE SAFE, AND TO OFFER YOU ANY HELP THAT I CAN.
I SHALL THINK MORE KINDLY OF DWARVES AFTER THIS. KILLED THE GREAT GOBLIN, KILLED THE GREAT GOBLIN!
WHAT DID YOU DO WITH THE GOBLIN AND THE WARG?
COME AND SEE!
Beorn was a fierce enemy. But now he was their friend and Gandalf thought it wise to tell him their whole story and the reason of their journey, so that they could get the most help he could offer.
This is what he promised to do for them. He would provide ponies for each of them, and a horse for Gandalf, and he would lade them with food to last them for weeks with care.
BUT YOUR WAY THROUGH MIRKWOOD IS DARK AND DANGEROUS AND DIFFICULT. WATER IS NOT EASY TO FIND. I WILL PROVIDE YOU WITH SKINS FOR CARRYING WATER. THERE IS ONE STREAM THERE, I KNOW, BLACK AND STRONG, WHICH CROSSES THE PATH. THAT YOU SHOULD NEITHER DRINK OF, NOR BATHE IN; FOR I HAVE HEARD THAT IT CARRIES ENCHANTMENT AND A GREAT DROWSINESS AND FORGETFULNESS.
AND NEVER LEAVE THE PATH. THAT YOU MUST NOT DO, FOR ANY REASON. THAT IS ALL THE ADVICE I CAN GIVE YOU. YOU MUST DEPEND ON YOUR LUCK AND YOUR COURAGE AND THE FOOD I SEND WITH YOU.

AT THE GATE OF THE FOREST I MUST ASK YOU TO SEND BACK MY HORSE AND MY PONIES. BUT I WISH YOU ALL SPEED, AND MY HOUSE IS OPEN TO YOU, IF EVER YOU COME BACK THIS WAY AGAIN.
WE ARE EVER AT YOUR SERVICE, O MASTER OF THE WIDE WOODEN HALLS!
By Beorn's advice they were no longer making for the main forest-road to the south of his land. He had warned them that that way was now often used by the goblins, while the forest-road itself, he had heard, was overgrown and disused at the eastern end and led to impassable marshes where the paths had long been lost.
Its eastern opening had also always been far to the south of the Lonely Mountain, and would have left them still with a long and difficult northward march when they got to the other side.
Beorn advised them to head north; for at a place a few days' ride due north of the Carrock was the gate of a little-known pathway through Mirkwood that led almost straight towards the Lonely Mountain.
"But I should ride fast," Beorn had said, "for if the goblins make their raid soon they will cross the river and scour all the edge of the forest so as to cut you off, and Wargs run swifter than ponies. Be off now as quick as you may!"
As the light faded Bilbo thought he saw the shadowy form of a great bear prowling along in the same direction. But if he dared to mention it to Gandalf, the wizard only said: "Hush! Take no notice!"
By the afternoon of the fourth day they had reached the eaves of Mirkwood, and were resting almost beneath the great over-hanging boughs of its outer trees.
WELL, HERE IS MIRKWOOD! THE GREATEST OF THE FORESTS OF THE NORTHERN WORLD. I HOPE YOU LIKE THE LOOK OF IT. NOW YOU MUST SEND BACK THESE EXCELLENT PONIES YOU HAVE BORROWED.
MUST WE SEND THEM BACK NOW? THERE IS SO MUCH TO CARRY.
BEORN IS NOT AS FAR OFF AS YOU SEEM TO THINK. MISTER BAGGINS' EYES ARE SHARPER THAN YOURS, IF YOU HAVE NOT SEEN EACH NIGHT AFTER DARK A GREAT BEAR GOING ALONG WITH US OR SITTING FAR OFF IN THE MOON WATCHING OUR CAMPS. NOT ONLY TO GUARD YOU AND GUIDE YOU, BUT TO KEEP AN EYE ON THE PONIES TOO.
YOU DO NOT GUESS WHAT WOULD HAPPEN TO YOU, IF YOU TRIED TO TAKE THEM INTO THE FOREST.

YOU DON'T MENTION SENDING THE HORSE BACK. WHAT ABOUT *YOUR* PROMISE THEN?
I WILL LOOK AFTER THAT. I AM NOT SENDING THE HORSE BACK, I AM RIDING IT!
THEN YOU REALLY MEAN TO LEAVE US AFTER ALL?

IT IS NO USE ARGUING. I HAVE, AS I TOLD YOU, SOME PRESSING BUSINESS AWAY SOUTH; AND I AM ALREADY LATE THROUGH BOTHERING WITH YOU PEOPLE. BUT I AM SENDING MISTER BAGGINS WITH YOU. I HAVE TOLD YOU BEFORE THAT HE HAS MORE ABOUT HIM THAN YOU GUESS, AND YOU WILL FIND THAT OUT BEFORE LONG.
SO CHEER UP THORIN AND COMPANY!
THIS IS YOUR EXPEDITION AFTER ALL. THINK OF THE TREASURE AT THE END!

So now there was nothing left to do but to fill their water-skins and unpack the ponies. They distributed the packages as fairly as they could, though Bilbo thought his lot was wearisomely heavy.
DON'T YOU WORRY! BEFORE LONG I EXPECT WE SHALL ALL WISH OUR PACKS HEAVIER, WHEN THE FOOD BEGINS TO RUN SHORT.

Then at last they said good-bye to their ponies who turned their heads for home. As they went away Bilbo could have sworn that a thing like a bear left the shadow of the trees and shambled off quickly after them.
GOOD-BYE TO YOU ALL, GOOD-BYE! STRAIGHT THROUGH THE FOREST IS YOUR WAY NOW. DON'T STRAY OFF THE TRACK!— IF YOU DO, IT IS A THOUSAND TO ONE YOU WILL NEVER FIND IT AGAIN AND NEVER GET OUT OF MIRKWOOD; AND THEN I DON'T SUPPOSE I, OR ANYONE ELSE, WILL EVER SEE YOU AGAIN.
DO WE REALLY HAVE TO GO THROUGH? I MEAN, IS THERE NO WAY ROUND?
YOU MUST EITHER GO THROUGH OR GIVE UP YOUR QUEST.
BEFORE YOU COULD GET ROUND MIRKWOOD IN THE NORTH YOU WOULD BE RIGHT AMONG THE SLOPES OF THE GREY MOUNTAINS, AND THEY ARE SIMPLY STIFF WITH GOBLINS, HOBGOBLINS, AND ORCS OF THE WORST DESCRIPTION.
BEFORE YOU COULD GET ROUND IT IN THE SOUTH, YOU WOULD GET INTO THE LAND OF THE NECROMANCER; AND EVEN YOU, BILBO, WON'T NEED ME TO TELL YOU TALES OF THAT BLACK SORCERER.
STICK TO THE FOREST TRACK, AND WITH A TREMENDOUS SLICE OF LUCK YOU *MAY* COME OUT ONE DAY AND SEE, HIGH IN THE EAST, THE LONELY MOUNTAIN WHERE DEAR OLD SMAUG LIVES, THOUGH I HOPE HE IS NOT EXPECTING YOU.
VERY COMFORTING YOU ARE TO BE SURE. GOOD-BYE! IF YOU WON'T COME WITH US, YOU HAD BETTER GET OFF WITHOUT ANY MORE TALK!
GOOD-BYE THEN, AND REALLY GOOD-BYE!
BE GOOD, TAKE CARE OF YOURSELVES — AND *DON'T LEAVE THE PATH!*

Soon the light at the gate to the forest was like a little bright hole far behind, and the quiet was so deep that their feet seemed to thump along while all the trees leaned over them and listened.
It was as dark in the forest in the morning as at night, and very secret: "a sort of watching and waiting feeling," Bilbo said to himself.
There were black squirrels in the wood and Bilbo caught glimpses of them scuttling behind tree trunks. There were queer noises too, grunts, scufflings, and hurryings in the undergrowth; but what made the noises even Bilbo's sharp inquisitive eyes could not see.
The nastiest things he and the dwarves saw were the cobwebs stretched from tree to tree. There were none across the path, but whether because some magic kept it clear, or for what other reason they could not guess.
It was not long before they grew to hate the forest as heartily as they had hated the tunnels of the goblins, and it seemed to offer even less hope of any ending. But they had to go on and on, long after they were sick for a sight of the sun and of the sky, and longed for the feel of wind on their faces.
The nights were the worst. It then became pitch-dark—not what you call pitch-dark, but really pitch; so black that you really could see nothing. Well, perhaps it is not true to say that they could see nothing: they could see eyes. And the eyes that Bilbo liked the least were horrible pale bulbous sort of eyes. "Insect eyes" he thought, "not animal eyes, only they are much too big."
As days followed days, and still the forest seemed just the same, they began to get anxious. The food would not last forever: it was in fact already beginning to get low. They tried shooting at the squirrels, and they wasted many arrows before they managed to bring one down on the path. But when they roasted it, it proved horrible to taste, and they shot no more squirrels.
They were thirsty too, for they had none too much water, and in all the time they had seen neither spring nor stream.

This was their state when one day they found their path blocked by a running water. It flowed fast and strong, and it was black, or looked it in the gloom.
It was well that Beorn had warned them against it, or they would have drunk from it, whatever its colour, and filled some of their emptied skins at its bank. As it was they only thought of how to cross it without wetting themselves in its water.
THERE IS A BOAT AGAINST THE FAR BANK!
NOW WHY COULDN'T IT HAVE BEEN ON THIS SIDE!
HOW FAR AWAY DO YOU THINK IT IS?
NOT AT ALL FAR, I SHOULDN'T THINK ABOVE TWELVE YARDS.
TWELVE YARDS! I SHOULD HAVE THOUGHT IT WAS THIRTY AT LEAST, BUT MY EYES DON'T SEE AS WELL AS THEY USED TO A HUNDRED YEARS AGO. WE CAN'T JUMP IT, AND WE DAREN'T TRY TO WADE OR SWIM.
CAN ANY OF YOU THROW A ROPE? I DON'T BELIEVE THE BOAT IS TIED, THOUGH OF COURSE I CAN'T BE SURE IN THIS LIGHT; BUT IT LOOKS TO ME AS IF IT WAS JUST DRAWN UP ON THE BANK.
Fili thought he could see the boat. So the others brought him a rope, and on the end they fastened one of the large iron hooks they had used for catching their packs to the straps about their shoulders.
CAREFULLY! IT IS LYING ON THE BOAT; LET'S HOPE THE HOOK WILL CATCH.
It did. The rope went taut, and Fili pulled in vain.
Kili came to his help, and then Oin and Gloin.
WHOA!
HELP!
OOOF!
IT WAS TIED AFTER ALL.
THAT WAS A GOOD PULL, MY LADS; AND A GOOD JOB THAT OUR ROPE WAS THE STRONGER.
WHO'LL CROSS FIRST?

I SHALL, AND YOU WILL COME WITH ME, AND FILI AND BALIN. THAT'S AS MANY AS THE BOAT WILL HOLD AT A TIME. AFTER THAT KILI AND OIN AND GLOIN AND DORI; NEXT ORI AND NORI, BIFUR AND BOFUR; AND LAST DWALIN AND BOMBUR.

I'M ALWAYS LAST AND I DON'T LIKE IT. IT'S SOMEBODY ELSE'S TURN TODAY.

YOU SHOULD NOT BE SO FAT. AS YOU ARE, YOU MUST BE WITH THE LAST AND LIGHTEST BOAT-LOAD. DON'T START GRUMBLING AGAINST ORDERS, OR SOMETHING BAD WILL HAPPEN TO YOU.

THERE AREN'T ANY OARS. HOW ARE YOU GOING TO PUSH THE BOAT BACK TO THE FAR BANK?

GIVE ME ANOTHER LENGTH OF ROPE AND ANOTHER HOOK.

GET IN NOW, AND ONE OF YOU HAUL ON THE ROPE I'VE THROWN INTO THE TREE ON THE OTHER SIDE. ONE OF THE OTHERS MUST KEEP HOLD OF THE HOOK WE USED AT FIRST, AND WHEN WE ARE SAFE ON THE OTHER SIDE HE CAN HOOK IT ON, AND YOU CAN DRAW THE BOAT BACK.

In this way they were all soon on the far bank safe across the enchanted stream...

...when something bad did happen.

THU-BA-TUP THU-BA-TUP THU-BA-TUP

Quickly they flung a rope with a hook towards him, and they pulled him to shore. He was drenched from hair to boots, of course, but that was not the worst.

When they laid him on the bank he was already fast asleep; and fast asleep he remained in spite of all they could do.
TA-RUMM
TA-RUMM
Then they became aware of the dim blowing of horns in the wood and the sound as of dogs baying far off.

Suddenly on the path ahead appeared some white deer, but before Thorin could cry out, the dwarves had loosed off their last arrows from their bows. None seemed to find their mark, and now the bows that Beorn had given them were useless.

They were a gloomy party that night, and the gloom gathered still deeper on them in the following days. Yet if they had known more about it and considered the meaning of the hunt and the white deer, they would have known that they were at last drawing towards the eastern edge of the forest.

But they did not know this, and they were burdened with the heavy body of Bombur, and in a few days a time came when there was practically nothing left to eat or drink. Nothing wholesome could they see growing in the woods, only funguses and herbs with pale leaves and unpleasant smell.

At times they heard disquieting laughter. Sometimes there was singing in the distance too. The laughter was the laughter of fair voices not of goblins, and the singing was beautiful, but it sounded eerie and strange, and they were not comforted, rather they hurried on from those parts with what strength they had left.

Two nights later, they ate their very last scraps and crumbs of food; and the next morning when they woke they noticed that they were still gnawingly hungry.
The only scrap of comfort there was, came unexpectedly from Bombur.
HUH?
Bombur could not make out where he was at all; for he had forgotten everything that had happened since they started their journey that May morning long ago. When he heard that there was nothing to eat, he wept.

WHY DID I EVER WAKE UP! I WAS HAVING SUCH BEAUTIFUL DREAMS. THERE WAS A WOODLAND KING WITH A CROWN OF LEAVES, AND THERE WAS A MERRY SINGING, AND I COULD NOT COUNT OR DESCRIBE THE THINGS THERE WERE TO EAT AND DRINK.
YOU NEED NOT TRY. IN FACT IF YOU CAN'T TALK ABOUT SOMETHING ELSE, YOU HAD BETTER BE SILENT.
WE ARE QUITE ANNOYED ENOUGH WITH YOU AS IT IS.

There was nothing now to be done but to tighten the belts round their empty stomachs, and trudge along the track without any great hope of ever getting to the end before they lay down and died of starvation.
WHAT WAS THAT? I THOUGHT I SAW A TWINKLE OF LIGHT IN THE FOREST.

IT LOOKS AS IF MY DREAMS WERE COMING TRUE. THERE MUST BE THINGS TO EAT AND DRINK THERE. LET'S GO SEE.
A FEAST WOULD BE NO GOOD, IF WE NEVER GOT BACK ALIVE FROM IT. GANDALF AND BEORN BOTH WARNED US ABOUT STRAYING FROM THE PATH.
BUT WITHOUT A FEAST WE SHAN'T REMAIN ALIVE MUCH LONGER ANYWAY.

They argued about it backwards and forwards for a long while. In the end, in spite of warnings, hunger decided them, because Bombur kept on describing all the good things that were being eaten, according to his dream, in the woodland feast; so they all plunged into the forest together.
After a good deal of creeping and crawling they peered round the trunks. There were many people there, elvish-looking folk; but the most splendid sight of all: they were eating and drinking and laughing merrily.

NO RUSHING FORWARD! NO ONE IS TO STIR FROM HIDING TILL I SAY. I SHALL SEND MISTER BAGGINS ALONE FIRST TO TALK TO THEM. THEY WON'T BE FRIGHTENED OF HIM, AND ANY WAY I HOPE THEY WON'T DO ANYTHING NASTY TO HIM.

Before he had time to slip on his ring, Bilbo was pushed forward into the full blaze of the fire and torches.

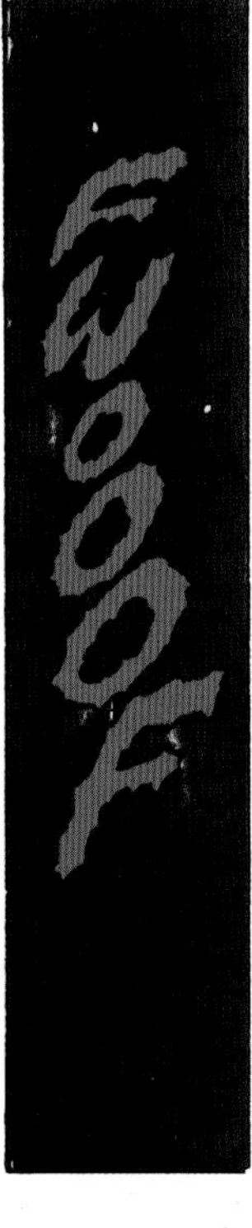

Out went all the lights as if by magic. They were lost in a completely lightless dark and they could not find one another, not for a long time at any rate, and of course they had quite forgotten in which direction the path lay.
BILBO BAGGINS! HOBBIT! YOU DRATTED HOBBIT!
HI! HOBBIT, CONFUSTICATE YOU, WHERE ARE YOU?
BILB-OH

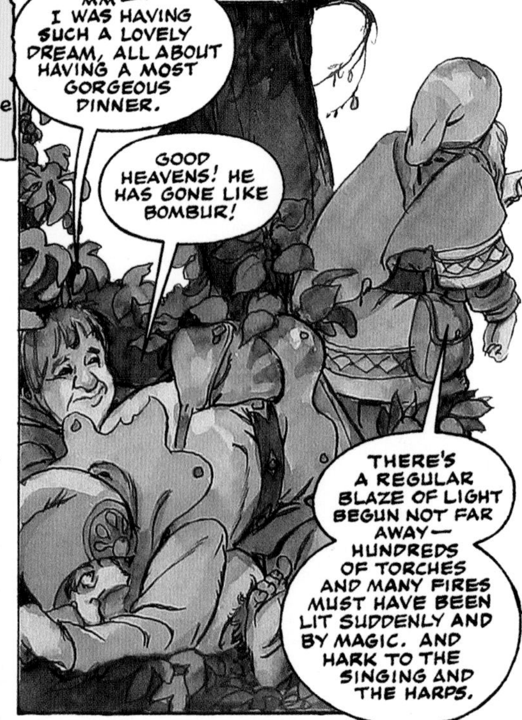

MM— I WAS HAVING SUCH A LOVELY DREAM, ALL ABOUT HAVING A MOST GORGEOUS DINNER.
GOOD HEAVENS! HE HAS GONE LIKE BOMBUR!
THERE'S A REGULAR BLAZE OF LIGHT BEGUN NOT FAR AWAY— HUNDREDS OF TORCHES AND MANY FIRES MUST HAVE BEEN LIT SUDDENLY AND BY MAGIC. AND HARK TO THE SINGING AND THE HARPS.

After lying and listening for a while, they found they could not resist the desire to go nearer and try once more to get help; and this time the result was disastrous.
The feast that they now saw was greater and more magnificent than before; and at the head of a long line of feasters stood a woodland king with a crown of leaves upon his golden hair, very much as Bombur had described the figure in his dream. The faces of the elvish folk and their songs were filled with mirth. Loud and clear and fair were those songs...
...and out stepped Thorin into their midst.
FWOOOF
Ashes and cinder were in the eyes of the dwarves, and the wood was filled again with their clamour and their cries.
DWALIN! BALIN! THORIN OAKENSHIELD!
OIN. GLOIN. FILI. KILI.
DORI? NORI? ORI?
BOMBUR! BIFUR! BOFUR!
The cries of the dwarves got steadily further and fainter. After a while it seemed to him they changed to yells and cries for help in the far distance, then he was left alone in complete silence and darkness.
That was one of Bilbo's most miserable moments. But he soon made up his mind that it was no good trying to do anything till day came with some little light. Not for the last time he fell to thinking of his far-distant hobbit-hole with its beautiful pantries.
AAA!
THOK

Somehow the killing of the giant spider, all alone by himself in the dark without the help of the wizard or the dwarves or of anyone else, made a great difference to Mister Baggins. He felt a different person, and much fiercer and bolder in spite of an empty stomach.
I WILL GIVE YOU A NAME AND I SHALL CALL YOU STING.
After that he set out to explore. He made as good a guess as he could at the direction from which the cries for help had come in the night— and by luck (he was born with a good share of it) he guessed more or less right, as you will see.
He crept along as cleverly as he could; also he slipped on his ring. That is why the spiders neither saw nor heard him coming.
IT WAS A SHARP STRUGGLE, BUT WORTH IT. WHAT NASTY THICK SKINS THEY HAVE TO BE SURE, BUT I'LL WAGER THERE IS GOOD JUICE INSIDE.
AYE, THEY'LL MAKE FINE EATING, WHEN THEY'VE HUNG A BIT.
DON'T HANG 'EM TOO LONG. THEY'RE NOT AS FAT AS THEY MIGHT BE. BEEN FEEDING NONE TOO WELL OF LATE, I SHOULD GUESS.
KILL 'EM, I SAY. KILL 'EM NOW AND HANG 'EM DEAD FOR A WHILE.
THEY'RE DEAD NOW, I'LL WARRANT.
THAT THEY ARE NOT. I SAW ONE A-STRUGGLING JUST NOW. JUST COMING ROUND AGAIN, I SHOULD SAY, AFTER A BEEAUTIFUL SLEEP. I'LL SHOW YOU.

MMRMPH
IT IS POOR OLD BOMBUR, I'LL BET.
PHUD
YOU WERE QUITE RIGHT. THE MEAT'S ALIVE AND KICKING!
I'LL SOON PUT AN END TO THAT.
KLAP
KLOP
After the two spiders fell dead there was a deal of commotion in the spider-colony, and they forgot the dwarves for a bit, I can tell you. They could not see Bilbo, but they could make a good guess at the direction from which the stones were coming.
Bilbo, however, soon slipped away to a different place. The idea came to him to lead the furious spiders further and further away from the dwarves, if he could.

OLD FAT SPIDER SPINNING IN A TREE! OLD FAT SPIDER CAN'T SEE ME! ATTERCOP! ATTERCOP! WON'T YOU STOP, STOP YOUR SPINNING AND LOOK AT ME!
WHUCK
OLD TOMNODDY, ALL BIG BODY, OLD TOMNODDY CAN'T SPY ME! ATTERCOP! ATTERCOP! DOWN YOU DROP! YOU'LL NEVER CATCH ME UP YOUR TREE!
Not very good perhaps, but then you must remember that he had to make it up himself, on the spur of a very awkward moment. It did what he wanted anyway.

The spiders made for his noise far quicker than he had expected. They were frightfully angry. Quite apart from the stones no spider has ever liked being called Attercop, and Tomnoddy of course is insulting to anybody.

The whole lot of them came hurrying after the hobbit along the ground and the branches, hairy legs waving, nippers and spinners snapping, eyes popping, full of froth and rage.

They followed him into the forest until Bilbo had gone as far as he dared. Then quieter than mouse he stole back.

Bilbo had precious little time, he knew, before the spiders were disgusted and came back to their trees where the dwarves were hung. In the meanwhile he had to rescue them.

Somehow or other Fili was got on to the branch, and then he did his best to help the hobbit, although he was feeling very sick and ill from spider-poison.

None of the other dwarves were better off than Fili, and some of them were worse... and there were still five dwarves hanging at the end of the branch when the spiders began to come back.
NOW WE SEE YOU, YOU NASTY LITTLE CREATURE! WE WILL EAT YOU AND LEAVE YOUR BONES AND SKIN HANGING ON A TREE.
UGH! HE'S GOT A STING HAS HE! WELL, WE'LL GET HIM ALL THE SAME, AND THEN WE'LL HANG HIM HEAD DOWNWARDS FOR A DAY OR TWO.

COME DOWN! COME DOWN! I AM GOING TO DISAPPEAR.
I SHALL DRAW THE SPIDERS OFF, IF I CAN; AND YOU MUST KEEP TOGETHER AND MAKE IN THE OPPOSITE DIRECTION. TO THE LEFT THERE, THAT IS MORE OR LESS THE WAY TOWARDS THE PLACE WHERE WE LAST SAW THE ELF-FIRES.

WHERE HAS MISTER BAGGINS GONE?
I DON'T KNOW. BUT HURRY AND DO AS HE SAID OR WE SHALL ALL BE NETTED.
LAZY LOB AND CRAZY COB ARE WEAVING WEBS TO WIND ME. I AM FAR MORE SWEET THAN OTHER MEAT, BUT STILL THEY CANNOT FIND ME.
KEEP A-SINGING, AND WE'LL FIND YOU...

...YET! AURK!
THOK

GO ON! GO ON! I WILL DO THE STINGING!
And he did. He hacked their legs, and stabbed their fat bodies if they came too near. The spiders swelled with rage, and spluttered and frothed, and hissed out horrible curses; but they had become mortally afraid of Sting, and dared not come very near.
THAK
So curse as they would, their prey moved steadily away. Just when Bilbo felt that he could not lift his hand for a single stroke more, the spiders suddenly gave it up, and followed them no more, but went back disappointed to their dark colony.

The dwarves soon began to ask questions. They had to have the whole vanishing business carefully explained, and the finding of the ring interested them so much that for a while they forgot their own troubles.
GOLLUM? WELL I'M BLEST! NOW I KNOW! BUTTONS ALL OVER THE DOORSTEP! GOOD OLD BILBO—BILBO — BO— bo — bo —
Knowing the truth about the vanishing did not lessen their opinion of Bilbo at all; for they saw that he had some wits, as well as luck and a magic ring — and all three are very useful possessions.

WHERE IS THORIN?
It was a terrible shock. Of course there were only thirteen of them, twelve dwarves and the hobbit. Where indeed was Thorin? They wondered what evil fate had befallen him, magic or dark monsters; and shuddered as they lay lost in the forest; and there we must leave them for the present, too sick and weary to set guards or take turns watching.

Thorin had been caught much faster than they had. You remember Bilbo falling like a log into sleep, as he stepped into the light of the elven fires and torches? The next time it had been Thorin who stepped forward, and as the lights went out he fell like a stone enchanted. All the sounds of the battle had passed over him unheard. Then the Wood-elves had come to him, and bound him, and carried him away.

The feasting people were Wood-elves, of course. These are not wicked folk. If they have a fault it is distrust of strangers. Though their magic was strong, even in those days they were wary.
They differed from the High Elves of the West, and were more dangerous and less wise. For most of them (together with their scattered relations in the hills and mountains) were descended from the ancient tribes that never went to Faerie in the West.
The subjects of the king mostly lived and hunted in the open woods, and had houses or huts on the ground and in the branches. The beeches were their favourite trees. The king's cave was his palace, and the strong place of his treasure, and the fortress of his people against their enemies.

It was also the dungeon of his prisoners. So to the cave they dragged Thorin — not too gently, for they did not love dwarves, and thought he was an enemy. In ancient days they had had wars with some of the dwarves, whom they accused of stealing their treasure.

It is only fair to say that the dwarves gave a different account, and Thorin's family had had nothing to do with the old quarrel I have spoken of.

Consequently Thorin was angry at their treatment of him, when they took their spell off him and he came to his senses; and also he was determined that no word of gold or jewels should be dragged out of him.

WHY DID YOU AND YOUR FOLK TWICE TRY TO ATTACK MY PEOPLE AT THEIR MERRY-MAKING?
WE DID NOT ATTACK THEM. WE CAME TO BEG, BECAUSE WE WERE STARVING.
WHERE ARE YOUR FRIENDS NOW, AND WHAT ARE THEY DOING?
I DON'T KNOW, BUT I EXPECT STARVING IN THE FOREST.
WHAT WERE YOU DOING IN THE FOREST?
LOOKING FOR FOOD AND DRINK, BECAUSE WE WERE STARVING.
BUT WHAT BROUGHT YOU INTO THE FOREST AT ALL?
VERY WELL! TAKE HIM AWAY AND KEEP HIM SAFE, UNTIL HE FEELS INCLINED TO TELL THE TRUTH. EVEN IF HE WAITS A HUNDRED YEARS.
There in the king's dungeon poor Thorin lay; and after he had got over his thankfulness for bread and meat and water, he began to wonder what had become of his unfortunate friends. It was not very long before he discovered.

The day after the battle with the spiders Bilbo and the dwarves made one last despairing effort to find a way out before they died of hunger and thirst. They got up and staggered on in the direction which eight out of the thirteen of them guessed to be the one in which the path lay; but they never found out if they were right.

There was no thought of a fight. Even if the dwarves had not been in such a state that they were actually glad to be captured, their small knives, the only weapons they had, would have been of no use against the arrows of the elves that could hit a bird's eye in the dark.

Bilbo popped on his ring and slipped quickly to one side. That is why the elves never found or counted the hobbit.

Each dwarf was blindfolded, but that did not make much difference, for even Bilbo with the use of his eyes could not see where they were going, and neither he nor the others knew where they had started from anyway.

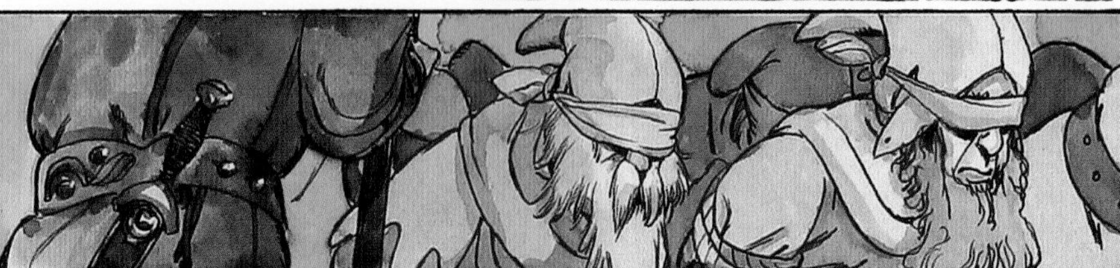

Across the bridge that led to the king's doors the elves thrust their prisoners, but Bilbo hesitated in the rear. He only made up his mind not to desert his friends just in time to scuttle over at the heels of the last elves, before the great gates of the king closed behind them with a clang.

UNBIND THEM. THEY NEED NO ROPES IN HERE. THERE IS NO ESCAPE FROM MY MAGIC DOORS FOR THOSE WHO ARE ONCE BROUGHT INSIDE.

WHAT HAVE WE DONE, O KING? IS IT A CRIME TO BE LOST IN THE FOREST, TO BE HUNGRY AND THIRSTY, TO BE TRAPPED BY SPIDERS? ARE THE SPIDERS YOUR TAME BEASTS OR YOUR PETS, IF KILLING THEM MAKES YOU ANGRY?

IT IS A CRIME TO WANDER IN MY REALM, WITHOUT LEAVE, USING THE ROAD THAT MY PEOPLE MADE. DID YOU NOT PURSUE AND TROUBLE MY PEOPLE IN THE FOREST AND ROUSE THE SPIDERS WITH YOUR RIOT AND CLAMOUR?
AFTER ALL THE DISTURBANCE YOU HAVE MADE I HAVE A RIGHT TO KNOW WHAT BRINGS YOU HERE, AND IF YOU WILL NOT TELL ME NOW, I WILL KEEP YOU ALL IN PRISON, IN SEPARATE CELLS, UNTIL YOU HAVE LEARNED SENSE AND MANNERS!

Poor Mister Baggins—it was a weary long time that he lived in that place all alone, and always in hiding, never daring to take off his ring, hardly daring to sleep, even tucked away in the darkest and remotest corners he could find. For something to do he took to wandering about the Elvenking's palace.

I AM LIKE A BURGLAR THAT CAN'T GET AWAY, BUT MUST GO ON MISERABLY BURGLING THE SAME HOUSE DAY AFTER DAY.

THIS IS THE DREARIEST AND DULLEST PART OF ALL THIS WRETCHED, TIRESOME, UNCOMFORTABLE ADVENTURE! I WISH I WAS BACK IN MY HOBBIT-HOLE BY MY OWN WARM FIRESIDE WITH THE LAMP SHINING.

He often wished, too, that he could get a message for help sent to the wizard, but that of course was quite impossible; and he soon realized that if anything was to be done, it would have to be done by Mister Baggins, alone and unaided.

Eventually, after a week or two of this sneaking sort of life, by watching and following the guards, he managed to find out where each dwarf was kept. What was his surprise one day to learn that there was another dwarf in prison too, in a specially deep dark place.

He guessed at once, of course, that that was Thorin; and after a while he found that his guess was right.

Thorin had a long whispered talk with the hobbit, and so it was that Bilbo was able to take secretly Thorin's message to each of the other imprisoned dwarves, telling them that Thorin their chief was also in prison close at hand, and that no one was to reveal their errand to the king, not yet, not before Thorin gave the word.

For Thorin had taken heart again hearing how the hobbit had rescued his companions from the spiders, and was determined not to ransom himself with promises to the king of a share in the treasure, until all hope of escaping in any other way had disappeared—

—until in fact the remarkable Mister Invisible Baggins (of whom he began to have a very high opinion indeed) had altogether failed to think of something clever.

The other dwarves quite agreed when they got the message.

Bilbo, however, did not feel so hopeful as they did. He sat and thought and thought, until his head nearly burst, but no bright idea would come. One invisible ring was a very fine thing, but it was not much good among fourteen.

But of course, as you have guessed, he did rescue his friends in the end, and this is how it happened.

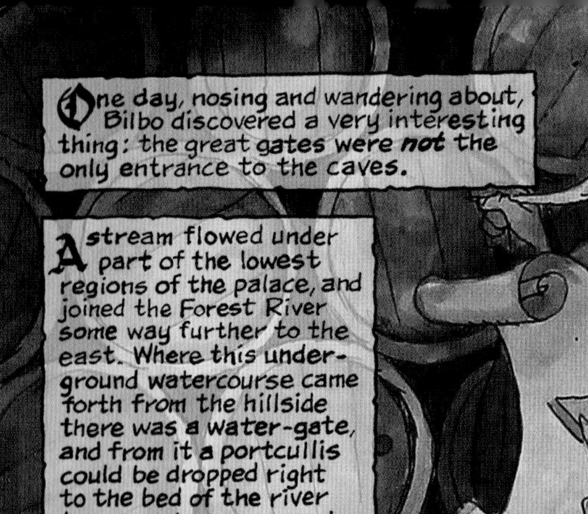

One day, nosing and wandering about, Bilbo discovered a very interesting thing: the great gates were *not* the only entrance to the caves.
A stream flowed under part of the lowest regions of the palace, and joined the Forest River some way further to the east. Where this underground watercourse came forth from the hillside there was a water-gate, and from it a portcullis could be dropped right to the bed of the river to prevent anyone coming in or out that way.

But at one point where the stream passed under the caves the roof had been cut away and covered with great oaken trapdoors. These opened upwards into the king's cellars, where wine, and other goods, were brought in barrels from far away, from their kinsfolk in the South, or from the vineyards of Men in distant lands.

When the barrels were empty the elves cast them through the trapdoors, opened the water-gate, and out the barrels floated on the stream, bobbing along, until they were carried by the current to a place far down the river near to the very eastern edge of Mirkwood. There they were collected and tied together and floated back to Lake-town—

—a town of Men, built out on bridges far into the water as a protection against enemies of all sorts, and especially against the dragon of the Mountain.

For some time Bilbo sat and thought about this water-gate, and wondered if it could be used for the escape of his friends, and at last he had the desperate beginnings of a plan.

NOW COME WITH ME AND TASTE THE NEW WINE THAT HAS JUST COME IN. I SHALL BE HARD AT WORK TONIGHT CLEARING THE CELLARS OF THE EMPTY WOOD, SO LET US HAVE A DRINK FIRST TO HELP THE LABOUR.
VERY GOOD. I'LL TASTE WITH YOU, AND SEE IF IT IS FIT FOR THE KING'S TABLE. THERE IS A FEAST TONIGHT AND IT WOULD NOT DO TO SEND UP POOR STUFF!

Luck of an unusual kind was with Bilbo then. It must be potent wine to make a wood-elf drowsy; but this wine, it would seem, was the heady vintage of the great gardens of Dorwinion, not meant for his soldiers or his servants, but for the king's feasts only, and for smaller bowls, not for the butler's great flagons.

First Bilbo unlocked Balin's door, and locked it again carefully as soon as the dwarf was outside.
YOU MUST FOLLOW ME! ALL OF US MUST ESCAPE OR NONE, AND THIS IS OUR LAST CHANCE. IF THIS IS FOUND OUT, GOODNESS KNOWS WHERE THE KING WILL PUT YOU NEXT. DON'T ARGUE, THERE'S A GOOD FELLOW!
Then off he went from door to door, until his following had grown to twelve. At last after much blundering they came to Thorin's dungeon, far down in a deep place and fortunately not far from the cellars.
UPON MY WORD! GANDALF SPOKE TRUE, AS USUAL. A PRETTY FINE BURGLAR YOU MAKE, IT SEEMS, WHEN THE TIME COMES.
I AM SURE WE ARE ALL FOR EVER AT YOUR SERVICE, WHATEVER HAPPENS AFTER THIS. BUT WHAT COMES NEXT?
Bilbo saw that the time had come to explain his idea as far as he would; but he did not feel at all sure how the dwarves would take it. His fears were quite justified, for they did not like it a bit.
WE SHALL BE BRUISED AND BATTERED TO PIECES, AND DROWNED TOO, FOR CERTAIN!
WE THOUGHT YOU HAD GOT SOME SENSIBLE NOTION, WHEN YOU MANAGED TO GET HOLD OF THE KEYS.
THIS IS A MAD IDEA!
VERY WELL! COME ALONG BACK TO YOUR NICE CELLS, AND I WILL LOCK YOU ALL IN AGAIN, AND YOU CAN SIT THERE COMFORTABLY AND THINK OF A BETTER PLAN — BUT I DON'T SUPPOSE I SHALL EVER GET HOLD OF THE KEYS AGAIN, EVEN IF I FEEL INCLINED TO TRY.
That was too much for them, and they calmed down. So following the hobbit, down into the lowest cellars they crept...
...but as they passed by the snoring guard, Bilbo stole in and kindheartedly put the keys back on his belt.
THAT WILL SAVE HIM SOME OF THE TROUBLE HE IS IN FOR. HE WASN'T A BAD FELLOW AND QUITE DECENT TO THE PRISONERS. IT WILL PUZZLE THEM ALL TOO. THEY WILL THINK WE HAD A VERY STRONG MAGIC TO PASS THROUGH ALL THOSE LOCKED DOORS AND DISAPPEAR.
DISAPPEAR!
WE HAVE GOT TO GET BUSY VERY QUICK, IF THAT IS TO HAPPEN.

There was little time to lose. Before long, as Bilbo knew, some elves were under orders to come down and help the butler get the empty barrels through the doors into the stream.
Some of them were wine-barrels, and these were not much use, as they could not easily be opened at the end without a deal of noise, nor could they easily be secured again. But among them were several others which had been used for bringing other stuffs, butter, apples, and all sorts of things, to the king's palace.
They soon found thirteen with room enough for a dwarf in each.
Bilbo did his best to find straw and other stuff to pack them in as cosily as could be managed in a short time.
Balin, who came last, made a great fuss about his air-holes and said he was stifling, even before his lid was on.
WHERE'S OLD GALION, THE BUTLER? I HAVEN'T SEEN HIM AT THE TABLES TONIGHT. HE OUGHT TO BE HERE NOW TO SHOW US WHAT IS TO BE DONE.
I SHALL BE ANGRY IF THE OLD SLOWCOACH IS LATE. I HAVE NO WISH TO WASTE TIME DOWN HERE WHILE THE SONG IS UP!
HA, HA! HERE'S THE OLD VILLAIN WITH HIS HEAD ON A JUG! HE'S BEEN HAVING A LITTLE FEAST ALL TO HIMSELF AND HIS FRIEND THE CAPTAIN.
SHAKE HIM! WAKE HIM!
YOU'RE ALL LATE. HERE AM I WAITING AND WAITING DOWN HERE, WHILE YOU FELLOWS DRINK AND MAKE MERRY AND FORGET YOUR TASKS. SMALL WONDER IF I FALL ASLEEP FROM *WEARINESS!*
SMALL WONDER, WHEN THE EXPLANATION STANDS CLOSE AT HAND IN A JUG!
SAVE US, GALION! YOU BEGAN YOUR FEASTING EARLY AND MUDDLED YOUR WITS! YOU HAVE STACKED SOME FULL CASKS HERE INSTEAD OF THE EMPTY ONES, IF THERE IS ANYTHING IN WEIGHT.
GET ON WITH THE WORK! THERE IS NOTHING IN THE FEELING OF WEIGHT IN AN IDLE TOSS-POT'S ARMS. THESE ARE THE ONES TO GO AND NO OTHERS. DO AS I SAY!
VERY WELL, VERY WELL! ON YOUR HEAD BE IT, IF THE KING'S FULL BUTTERTUBS AND HIS BEST WINE IS PUSHED INTO THE RIVER FOR THE LAKE-MEN TO FEAST ON FOR NOTHING!
ROLL-ROLL-ROLL-ROLL, ROLL-ROLL-ROLLING DOWN THE HOLE! HEAVE HO! SPLASH PLUMP! DOWN THEY GO, DOWN THEY BUMP!

It was just at this moment that Bilbo suddenly discovered the weak point in his plan. Most likely you saw it some time ago and have been laughing at him; but I don't suppose you would have done half as well yourselves in his place. Of course *he* was not in a barrel himself, nor was there anyone to pack him in, even if there had been a chance!

Now the very last barrel was being rolled to the doors! In despair and not knowing what else to do, poor little Bilbo caught hold of it and was pushed over the edge with it.

He came up again spluttering and clinging to the wood like a rat, but for all his efforts he could not scramble on top. He was in the dark tunnel, floating in icy water, all alone — for you cannot count friends that are all packed up in barrels.
POOOSHH

He heard the creak of the water-gate being hauled up, and he found that he was in the midst of a bobbing and bumping mass of casks and tubs all pressing together to pass under the arch and get out into the open stream.
I DO HOPE I PUT THE LIDS ON TIGHT ENOUGH!

Bilbo took the opportunity of scrambling up the side of his barrel while it was held steady against another. Up he crawled like a drowned rat, and lay on the top spread out to keep the balance as best he could.
The breeze was cold but better than the water, and he hoped he would not suddenly roll off again when they started off once more.

Luckily he was very light, and the barrel was a good big one and being rather leaky had now shipped a small amount of water. All the same it was like trying to ride, without bridle or stirrups, a round-bellied pony that was always thinking of rolling on the grass.

In this way at last Mister Baggins came to a place where the trees on either hand grew thinner. The dark river opened suddenly wide, and there it was joined to the main water of the Forest River flowing down in haste from the king's great doors.

There were people on the look-out on the banks. They quickly poled and pushed all the barrels together into the shallows, and when they had counted them they roped them together and left them till the morning.

Poor dwarves! Bilbo was not so badly off now. He slipped from his barrel and waded ashore. He no longer thought twice about picking up a supper uninvited if he got the chance, he had been obliged to do it for so long, and he knew only too well what it was to be really hungry.
There is no need to tell you much of his adventures that night, for now we are drawing near the end of the eastward journey and coming to the last and greatest adventure, so we must hurry on.
Very soon there was a fine commotion, but Bilbo escaped into the woods. The rest of the night he had to pass wet as he was and far from a fire, and he actually dozed a little on some dry leaves, even though the year was getting late and the air was chilly.
Of course helped by his magic ring he got on very well at first, but he was given away in the end by his wet footsteps and the trail of drippings that he left wherever he went or sat; and also he began to snivel, and he was found out by the terrific explosions of his suppressed sneezes.
Also he had caught a glimpse of a fire through the trees, and that appealed to him with his dripping and ragged clothes clinging to him cold and clammy.
He awoke again with a specially loud sneeze. It was already grey morning, and there was a merry racket down by the river.
They were making up a raft of barrels to steer down the stream to Lake-Town. Bilbo scrambled down as fast as his stiff legs would take him and managed just in time to get on to the mass of casks without being noticed in the general bustle.
THIS IS A HEAVY LOAD! THEY FLOAT TOO DEEP—SOME OF THESE ARE NEVER EMPTY. IF THEY HAD COME ASHORE IN THE DAYLIGHT, WE MIGHT HAVE HAD A LOOK INSIDE.
NO TIME NOW! SHOVE OFF!
And off they went at last, slowly at first, and then quicker and quicker as they caught the main stream and went sailing away down, down towards the Lake.
They had escaped the dungeons of the king and were through the wood, but whether alive or dead still remains to be seen.

The day grew lighter and warmer as they floated along.
After a while the river rounded a steep shoulder of land that came down upon their left. Under its rocky feet like an inland cliff the deepest stream had flowed lapping and bubbling.
Suddenly the cliff fell away. The shores sank. The trees ended.
Then Bilbo saw a sight:
Far away, its dark head in a torn cloud, there loomed the Mountain! Its nearest neighbors to the North-East and the tumbled land that joined it to them could not be seen. All alone it rose and looked across the marshes to the forest.
The Lonely Mountain! Bilbo had come far and through many adventures to see it, and now he did not like the look of it in the least.

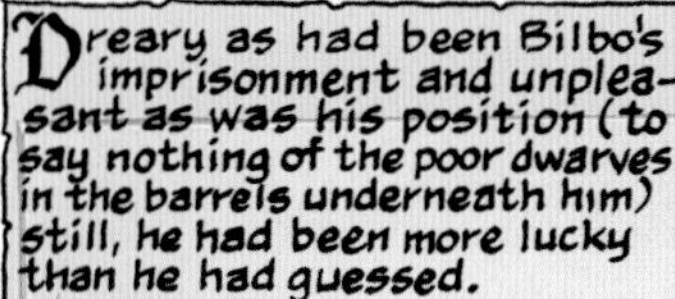
Dreary as had been Bilbo's imprisonment and unpleasant as was his position (to say nothing of the poor dwarves in the barrels underneath him) still, he had been more lucky than he had guessed.

The elf-road which the dwarves had followed now came to a doubtful and little used end at the eastern edge of the forest; only the river offered any longer a safe way from the skirts of Mirkwood in the North to the mountain-shadowed plains beyond.
So you see Bilbo had come in the end by the only road that was any good. But Bilbo did not know it.

All he knew was that the river seemed to go on and on and on for ever, and he was hungry, and had a nasty cold in the nose, and did not like the way the Mountain seemed to frown at him and threaten him as it drew ever nearer.

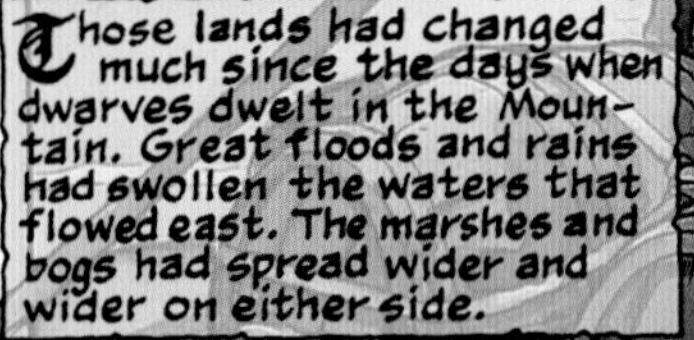
Those lands had changed much since the days when dwarves dwelt in the Mountain. Great floods and rains had swollen the waters that flowed east. The marshes and bogs had spread wider and wider on either side.

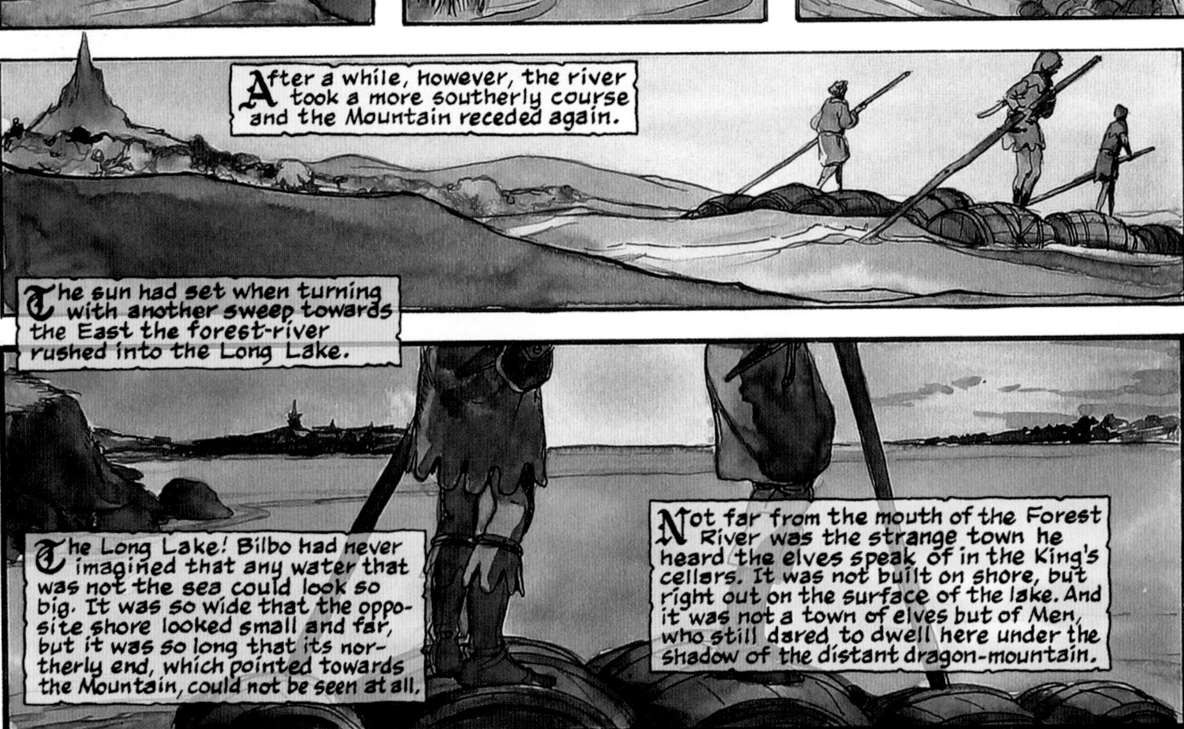
After a while, however, the river took a more southerly course and the Mountain receded again.
The sun had set when turning with another sweep towards the East the forest-river rushed into the Long Lake.
The Long Lake! Bilbo had never imagined that any water that was not the sea could look so big. It was so wide that the opposite shore looked small and far, but it was so long that its northerly end, which pointed towards the Mountain, could not be seen at all.
Not far from the mouth of the Forest River was the strange town he heard the elves speak of in the King's cellars. It was not built on shore, but right out on the surface of the lake. And it was not a town of elves but of Men, who still dared to dwell here under the shadow of the distant dragon-mountain.

They still throve on the trade that came up the great river from the South, but in the great days of old, when Dale in the North was rich and prosperous, they had been wealthy and powerful.
But men remembered little of all that, though some still sang old songs of the dwarf-kings of the Mountain and the coming of the Dragon. Some sang too that Thror and Thrain would come back one day and gold would flow in rivers through the mountain-gates. But this pleasant legend did not much affect their daily business.

As soon as the raft of barrels came in sight boats rowed out from the piles of the town, and voices hailed the raftsteerers, and the raft was drawn out of the current of the forest River and moored not far from the shoreward head of the great bridge which ran out to where the town was built.

Soon men would come up from the South and take some of the casks away, and others they would fill with goods they had brought to be taken back up the stream to the Wood-elves' home. In the meanwhile the barrels were left afloat while the elves of the raft and the boatmen went to feast in Lake-town.

They would have been surprised, if they could have seen what happened down by the shore, after they had gone and the shades of night had fallen.

UNNHHHH
WELL, ARE YOU ALIVE OR ARE YOU DEAD? IF YOU WANT FOOD, AND IF YOU WANT TO GO ON WITH THIS SILLY ADVENTURE — IT'S YOURS AFTER ALL AND NOT MINE — YOU HAD BETTER SLAP YOUR ARMS AND RUB YOUR LEGS AND TRY AND HELP ME GET THE OTHERS OUT WHILE THERE IS A CHANCE!

Thorin of course saw the sense of this, so after a few more groans he got up and helped the hobbit as well as he could. In the darkness, floundering in the cold water, they had a difficult and very nasty job finding which were the right barrels.

I HOPE I NEVER SMELL THE SMELL OF APPLES AGAIN! MY TUB WAS FULL OF IT! TO SMELL APPLES EVERLASTINGLY WHEN YOU CAN SCARCELY MOVE AND ARE COLD AND SICK WITH HUNGER IS MADDENING. I COULD EAT ANYTHING IN THE WIDE WORLD NOW, FOR HOURS ON END— BUT NOT AN APPLE!
Dwalin and Balin were two of the most unhappy. Bifur and Bofur were less knocked about and drier. Fili and Kili came out more or less smiling, with only a bruise or two.
Poor fat Bombur was asleep or senseless; Dori, Nori, Ori, Oin and Gloin were waterlogged and seemed only half alive; they all had to be carried one by one and laid helpless on the shore.

WELL! HERE WE ARE! AND I SUPPOSE WE OUGHT TO THANK OUR LUCKY STARS AND MISTER BAGGINS. I AM SURE HE HAS A RIGHT TO EXPECT IT, THOUGH I WISH HE COULD HAVE ARRANGED A MORE COMFORTABLE JOURNEY. STILL — ALL VERY MUCH AT YOUR SERVICE ONCE MORE, MISTER BAGGINS. NO DOUBT WE SHALL FEEL PROPERLY GRATEFUL, WHEN WE ARE FED AND RECOVERED.
IN THE MEANWHILE, WHAT NEXT?
I SUGGEST LAKE TOWN. WHAT ELSE IS THERE?

Nothing else could, of course, be suggested; so leaving the others, Thorin and Fili and Kili and the hobbit went along the shore to the great bridge.
There were guards at the head of it, but they were not keeping very careful watch, for it was so long since there had been any real need. That being so it is not surprising that the guards were drinking and laughing by a fire in their hut, and did not hear the noise of the unpacking of the dwarves.

WHO ARE YOU AND WHAT DO YOU WANT?
THORIN SON OF THRAIN SON OF THROR KING UNDER THE MOUNTAIN! I HAVE COME BACK. I WISH TO SEE THE MASTER OF YOUR TOWN!

There was tremendous excitement. Some of the more foolish ran out of the hut as if they expected the Mountain to go golden in the night and all the waters of the lake to turn yellow right away.
AND WHO ARE THESE?
THE SONS OF MY FATHER'S DAUGHTER, FILI AND KILI OF THE RACE OF DURIN, AND MISTER BAGGINS WHO HAS TRAVELLED WITH US OUT OF THE WEST.
IF YOU COME IN PEACE LAY DOWN YOUR ARMS!

And it was true enough; their knives had been taken from them by the Wood-elves, and the great sword Orcrist too.
WE HAVE NONE.
Bilbo had his short sword, hidden as usual, but he said nothing about that.

WE HAVE NO NEED OF WEAPONS, WHO RETURN AT LAST TO OUR OWN AS SPOKEN OF OLD. NOR COULD WE FIGHT AGAINST SO MANY.
TAKE US TO YOUR MASTER!

HE IS AT FEAST.
THEN ALL THE MORE REASON FOR TAKING US TO HIM. WE ARE WORN AND FAMISHED AFTER OUR LONG ROAD AND WE HAVE SICK COMRADES.
NOW MAKE HASTE. AND LET US HAVE NO MORE WORDS, OR YOUR MASTER MAY HAVE SOMETHING TO SAY TO YOU.

FOLLOW ME THEN.

I AM THORIN SON OF THRAIN SON OF THROR KING UNDER THE MOUNTAIN!
I RETURN!!
THESE ARE PRISONERS OF OUR KING THAT HAVE ESCAPED, WANDERING VAGABOND DWARVES THAT COULD NOT GIVE ANY GOOD ACCOUNT OF THEMSELVES, SNEAKING THROUGH THE WOODS AND MOLESTING OUR PEOPLE.
IS THIS TRUE?
IT IS TRUE THAT WE WERE WRONGFULLY WAY-LAID BY THE ELVEN-KING AND IMPRISONED WITHOUT CAUSE AS WE JOURNEYED BACK TO OUR OWN LAND.
BUT LOCK NOR BAR MAY HIN-DER THE HOMECOMING SPOKEN OF OLD. NOR IS THIS TOWN IN THE WOOD-ELVES' REALM. I SPEAK TO THE MASTER OF THE TOWN OF THE MEN OF THE LAKE, NOT TO THE RAFT-MEN OF THE KING.

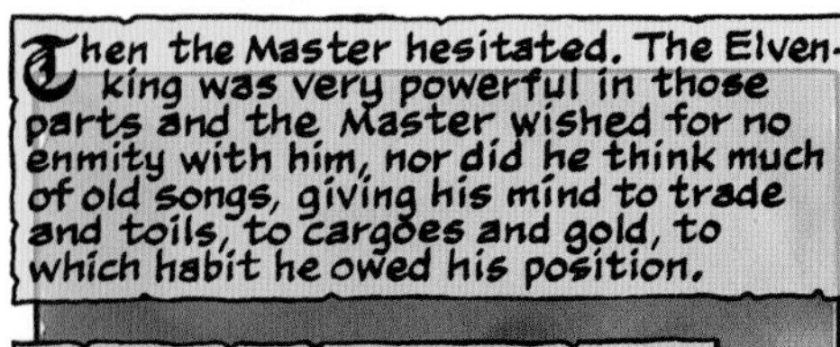
Then the Master hesitated. The Elvenking was very powerful in those parts and the Master wished for no enmity with him, nor did he think much of old songs, giving his mind to trade and tolls, to cargoes and gold, to which habit he owed his position.

Others were of different mind, however, and quickly the matter was settled without him.

THE KING BENEATH THE MOUNTAINS,
THE KING OF CARVEN STONE,
THE LORD OF SILVER FOUNTAINS
SHALL COME INTO HIS OWN
THE STREAMS SHALL RUN IN GLADNESS
THE LAKE SHALL SHINE AND BURN
AND SORROW FAIL AND SADNESS
AT THE MOUNTAIN-KING'S RETURN
That it was Thror's grandson not Thror himself that had come back did not bother them at all. And no explanation of where Bilbo came in — no songs had alluded to him even in the obscurest way — was asked for in the general bustle.

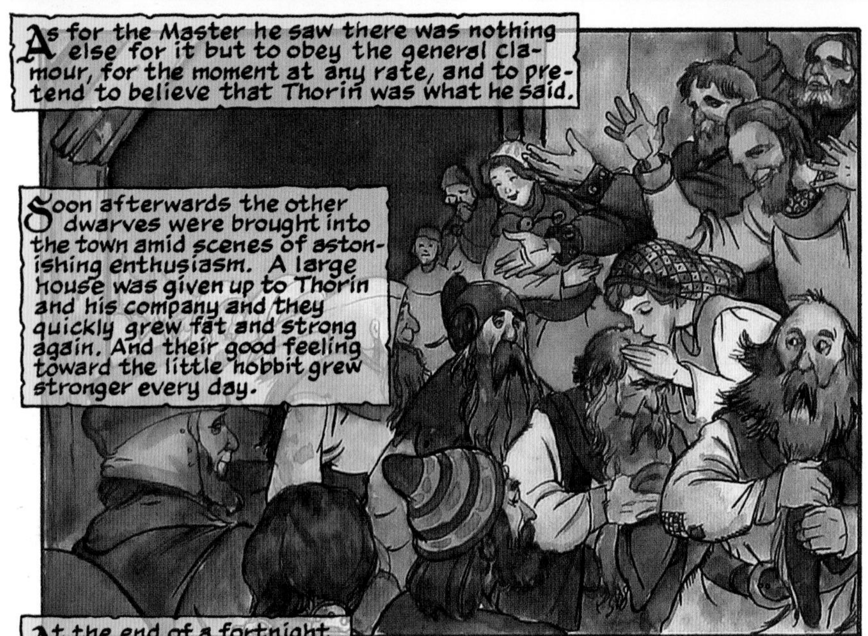
As for the Master he saw there was nothing else for it but to obey the general clamour, for the moment at any rate, and to pretend to believe that Thorin was what he said.
Soon afterwards the other dwarves were brought into the town amid scenes of astonishing enthusiasm. A large house was given up to Thorin and his company and they quickly grew fat and strong again. And their good feeling toward the little hobbit grew stronger every day.

But Bilbo had not forgotten the look of the Mountain, nor the thought of the dragon, and he had besides a shocking cold.
THAG YOU VERY BUCH.

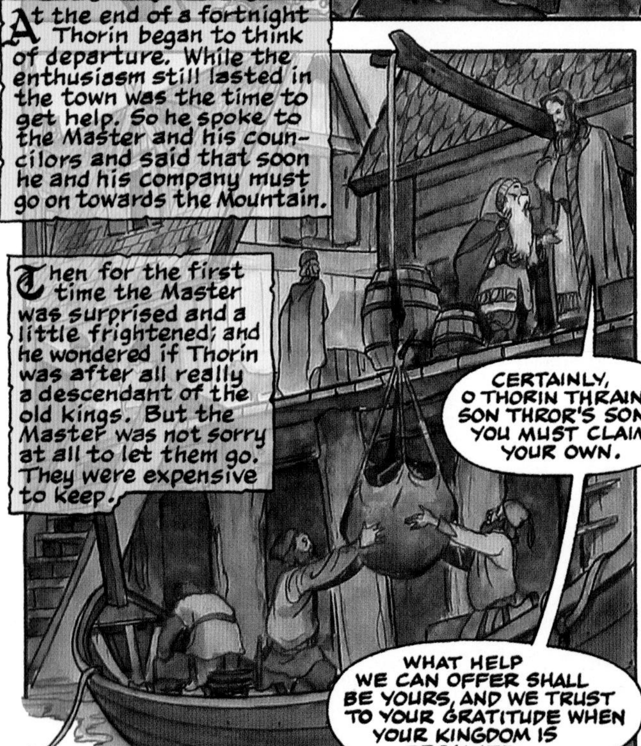
At the end of a fortnight Thorin began to think of departure. While the enthusiasm still lasted in the town was the time to get help. So he spoke to the Master and his councilors and said that soon he and his company must go on towards the Mountain.
Then for the first time the Master was surprised and a little frightened; and he wondered if Thorin was after all really a descendant of the old kings. But the Master was not sorry at all to let them go. They were expensive to keep.
CERTAINLY, O THORIN THRAIN'S SON THROR'S SON! YOU MUST CLAIM YOUR OWN.
WHAT HELP WE CAN OFFER SHALL BE YOURS, AND WE TRUST TO YOUR GRATITUDE WHEN YOUR KINGDOM IS REGAINED.

So one day, although autumn was now getting far on, and winds were cold, and leaves were falling fast, three large boats left Lake-town. Horses and ponies had been sent round by circuitous paths to meet them at their appointed landing-place.
The Master and his councilors bade them farewell. People sang on the quay and out of windows.
The only person thoroughly unhappy was Bilbo.

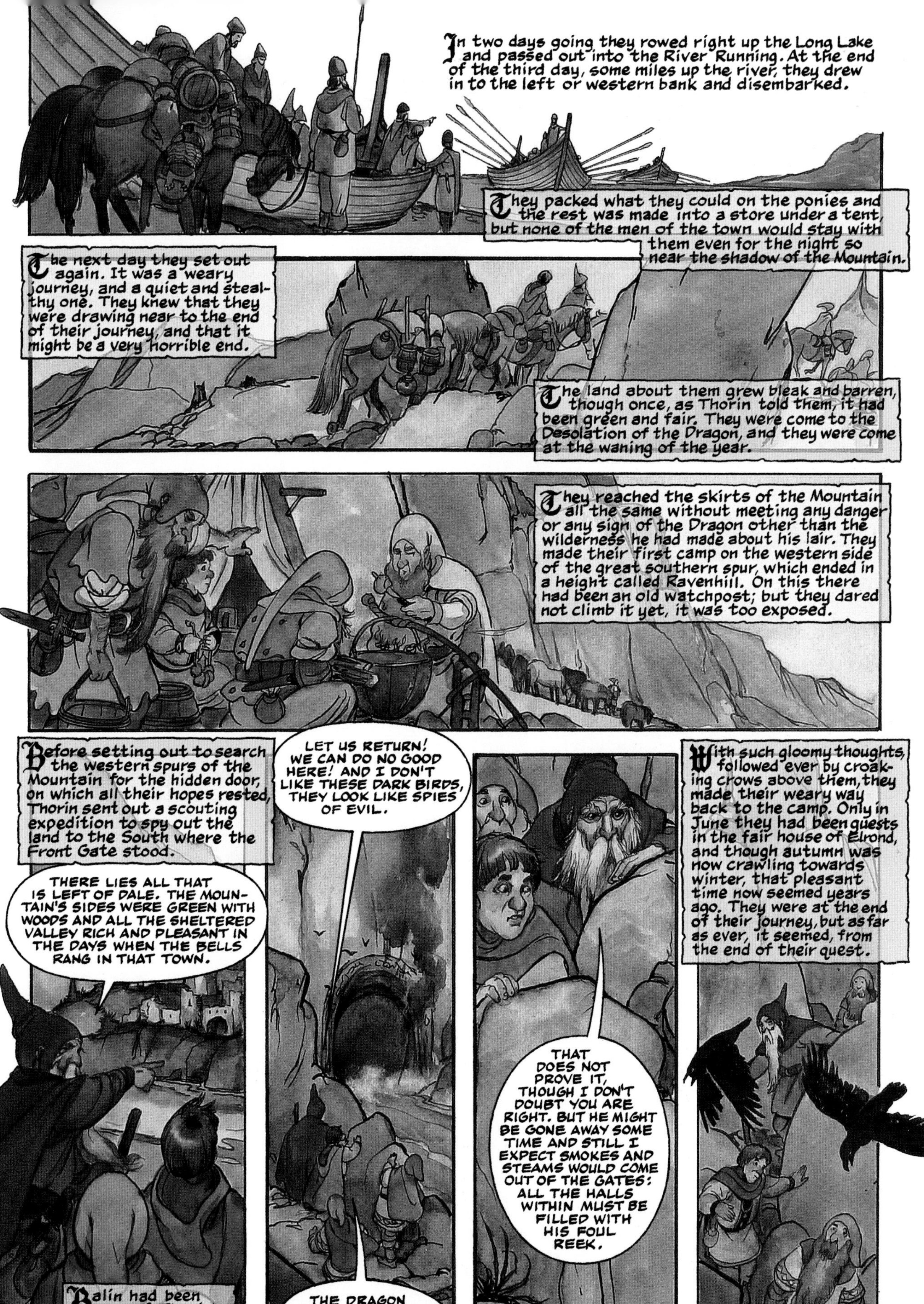
In two days going they rowed right up the Long Lake and passed out into the River Running. At the end of the third day, some miles up the river, they drew in to the left or western bank and disembarked.
They packed what they could on the ponies and the rest was made into a store under a tent, but none of the men of the town would stay with them even for the night so near the shadow of the Mountain.
The next day they set out again. It was a weary journey, and a quiet and stealthy one. They knew that they were drawing near to the end of their journey, and that it might be a very horrible end.
The land about them grew bleak and barren, though once, as Thorin told them, it had been green and fair. They were come to the Desolation of the Dragon, and they were come at the waning of the year.
They reached the skirts of the Mountain all the same without meeting any danger or any sign of the Dragon other than the wilderness he had made about his lair. They made their first camp on the western side of the great southern spur, which ended in a height called Ravenhill. On this there had been an old watchpost; but they dared not climb it yet, it was too exposed.
Before setting out to search the western spurs of the Mountain for the hidden door, on which all their hopes rested, Thorin sent out a scouting expedition to spy out the land to the South where the Front Gate stood.
THERE LIES ALL THAT IS LEFT OF DALE. THE MOUNTAIN'S SIDES WERE GREEN WITH WOODS AND ALL THE SHELTERED VALLEY RICH AND PLEASANT IN THE DAYS WHEN THE BELLS RANG IN THAT TOWN.
Balin had been one of Thorin's companions on the day the dragon came.
LET US RETURN! WE CAN DO NO GOOD HERE! AND I DON'T LIKE THESE DARK BIRDS, THEY LOOK LIKE SPIES OF EVIL.
THE DRAGON IS STILL ALIVE AND IN THE HALLS UNDER THE MOUNTAIN THEN—OR I IMAGINE SO FROM THE SMOKE.
THAT DOES NOT PROVE IT, THOUGH I DON'T DOUBT YOU ARE RIGHT. BUT HE MIGHT BE GONE AWAY SOME TIME AND STILL I EXPECT SMOKES AND STEAMS WOULD COME OUT OF THE GATES: ALL THE HALLS WITHIN MUST BE FILLED WITH HIS FOUL REEK.
With such gloomy thoughts, followed ever by croaking crows above them, they made their weary way back to the camp. Only in June they had been guests in the fair house of Elrond, and though autumn was now crawling towards winter, that pleasant time now seemed years ago. They were at the end of their journey, but as far as ever, it seemed, from the end of their quest.
None of them had much spirit left.

Now strange to say Mister Baggins had more than the others. He would often borrow Thorin's map and gaze at it, pondering over the runes and the message of the moon-letters Elrond had read.

It was he that made the dwarves begin the dangerous search on the western slopes for the secret door.

They moved their camp to the western side of the Mountain, where there were fewer signs of the dragon's marauding feet, and there was some grass for their ponies.
From this western camp, shadowed all day by cliff and wall until the sun began to sink towards the forest, day by day they toiled in parties searching for paths up the mountain-side. If the map was true, somewhere high above the cliff at the valley's head must stand the secret door.
Day by day they came back to their camp without success.

But at last unexpectedly they found what they were seeking. Bilbo with Fili and Kili found traces of a narrow track, often lost, often rediscovered, that wandered on to the top of the southern ridge and brought them at last to a still narrower ledge.

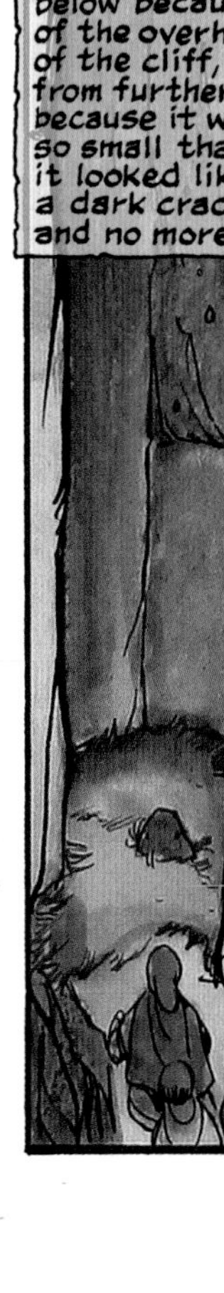

Looking down they saw that they were at the top of the cliff at the valley's head and were gazing down on to their own camp below.

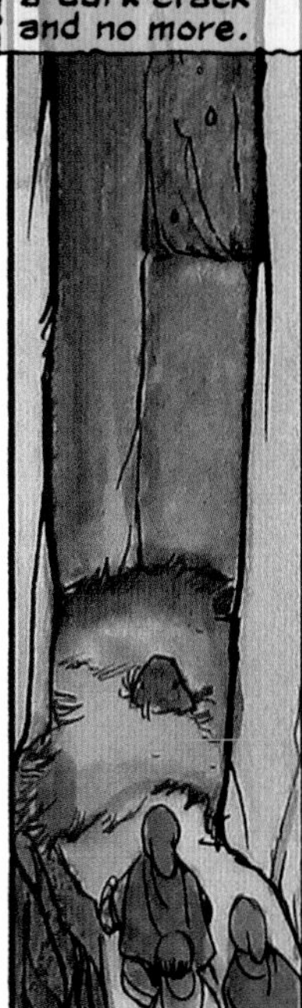

Then the wall opened and they turned into a little steep-walled bay, grassy-floored, still and quiet. Its entrance which they had found could not be seen from below because of the overhang of the cliff, nor from further off because it was so small that it looked like a dark crack and no more.

At its inner end a flat wall rose up that was as smooth and upright as mason's work, but without joint or crevice to be seen. No sign was there of post or lintel or threshold, nor any sign of bar or bolt or key-hole; yet they did not doubt that they had found the door at last.

They beat on it, they thrust and pushed at it, they implored it to move, they spoke fragments of broken spells of opening, and nothing stirred.

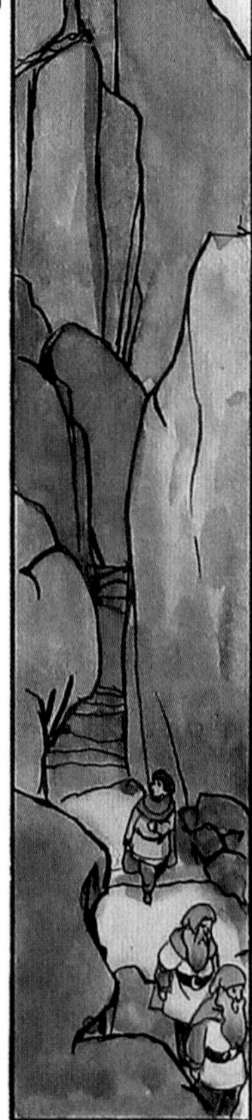

At last tired out they began their long climb down.

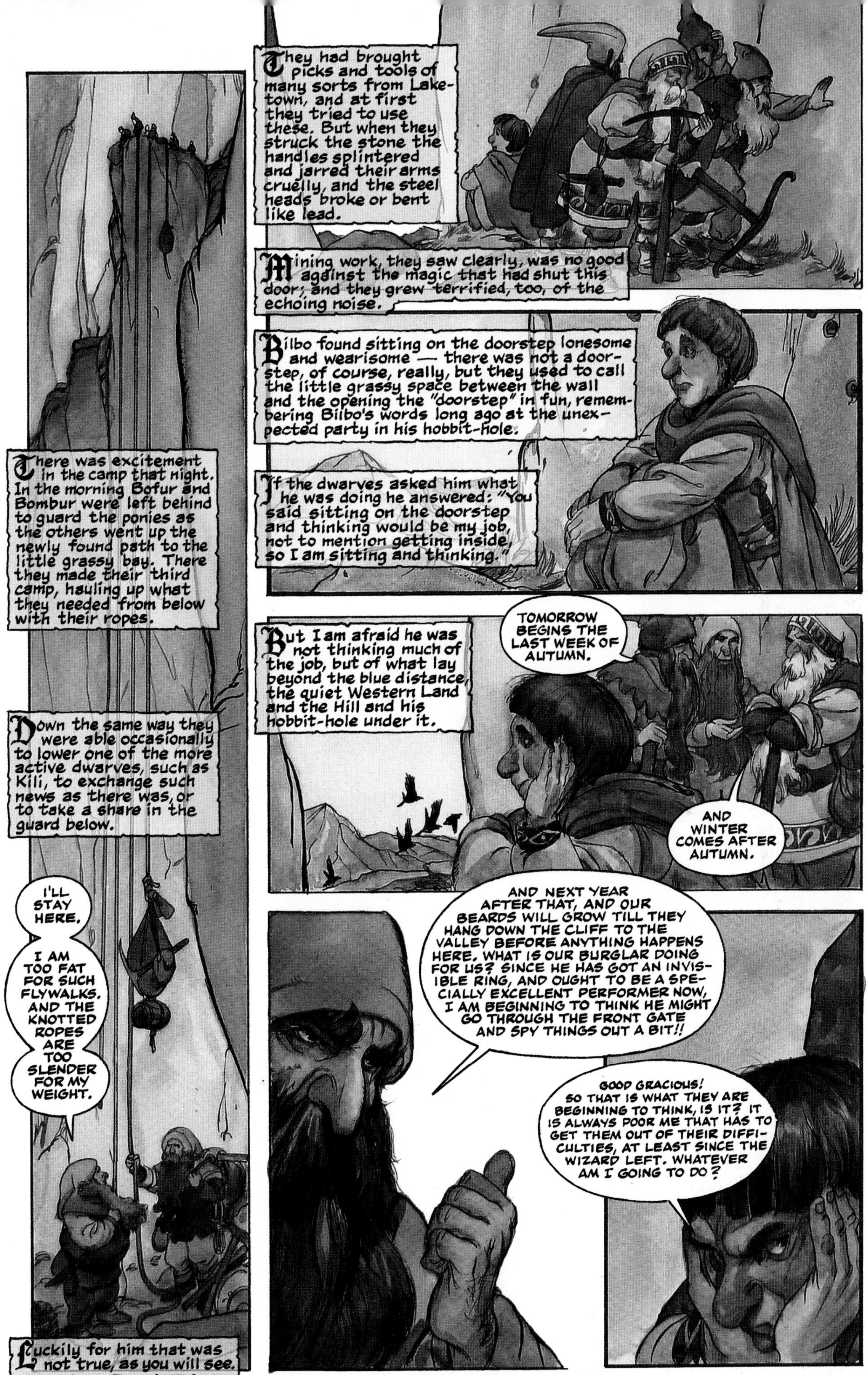

There was excitement in the camp that night. In the morning Bofur and Bombur were left behind to guard the ponies as the others went up the newly found path to the little grassy bay. There they made their third camp, hauling up what they needed from below with their ropes.

Down the same way they were able occasionally to lower one of the more active dwarves, such as Kili, to exchange such news as there was, or to take a share in the guard below.

I'LL STAY HERE.
I AM TOO FAT FOR SUCH FLYWALKS, AND THE KNOTTED ROPES ARE TOO SLENDER FOR MY WEIGHT.

Luckily for him that was not true, as you will see.

They had brought picks and tools of many sorts from Lake-town, and at first they tried to use these. But when they struck the stone the handles splintered and jarred their arms cruelly, and the steel heads broke or bent like lead.

Mining work, they saw clearly, was no good against the magic that had shut this door; and they grew terrified, too, of the echoing noise.

Bilbo found sitting on the doorstep lonesome and wearisome — there was not a door-step, of course, really, but they used to call the little grassy space between the wall and the opening the "doorstep" in fun, remembering Bilbo's words long ago at the unexpected party in his hobbit-hole.

If the dwarves asked him what he was doing he answered: "You said sitting on the doorstep and thinking would be my job, not to mention getting inside, so I am sitting and thinking."

But I am afraid he was not thinking much of the job, but of what lay beyond the blue distance, the quiet Western Land and the Hill and his hobbit-hole under it.

TOMORROW BEGINS THE LAST WEEK OF AUTUMN.

AND WINTER COMES AFTER AUTUMN.

AND NEXT YEAR AFTER THAT, AND OUR BEARDS WILL GROW TILL THEY HANG DOWN THE CLIFF TO THE VALLEY BEFORE ANYTHING HAPPENS HERE. WHAT IS OUR BURGLAR DOING FOR US? SINCE HE HAS GOT AN INVISIBLE RING, AND OUGHT TO BE A SPECIALLY EXCELLENT PERFORMER NOW, I AM BEGINNING TO THINK HE MIGHT GO THROUGH THE FRONT GATE AND SPY THINGS OUT A BIT!!

GOOD GRACIOUS! SO THAT IS WHAT THEY ARE BEGINNING TO THINK, IS IT? IT IS ALWAYS POOR ME THAT HAS TO GET THEM OUT OF THEIR DIFFICULTIES, AT LEAST SINCE THE WIZARD LEFT. WHATEVER AM I GOING TO DO?

KRAK

There on a grey stone in the center of the grass was an enormous thrush. It had caught a snail and was knocking it on the stone.
KRAK KRAK
Suddenly Bilbo understood.

Forgetting all danger he hailed the dwarves, shouting and waving. Those that were nearest came tumbling over the rocks and as fast as they could along the ledge to him, wondering what on earth was the matter.

Quickly Bilbo explained. They all fell silent.
The sun sank lower and lower, and their hopes fell. It sank into a belt of reddened cloud and disappeared. The dwarves groaned, but still Bilbo stood almost without moving.
Then suddenly when their hope was lowest a red ray of the sun escaped like a finger through a rent in the cloud. A gleam of light came straight through the opening into the bay and fell on the smooth rock face.

PIP
PIP
PIP
KRRAK

THE KEY! THE KEY! THE KEY THAT WENT WITH THE MAP! TRY IT NOW WHILE THERE IS STILL TIME!

Now they all pushed together, and slowly a part of the rock-wall gave way. Long straight cracks appeared and widened. A door five feet high and three broad was outlined, and slowly without a sound swung inwards.
KLAK
It seemed as if darkness flowed out like a vapour from the hole in the mountain-side, and deep darkness in which nothing could be seen lay before their eyes, a yawning mouth leading in and down.
NOW IS THE TIME FOR OUR ESTEEMED MISTER BAGGINS, WHO HAS PROVED HIMSELF A GOOD COMPANION ON OUR LONG ROAD, AND A HOBBIT FULL OF COURAGE AND RESOURCE FAR EXCEEDING HIS SIZE — NOW IS THE TIME FOR HIM TO PERFORM THE SERVICE FOR WHICH HE WAS INCLUDED IN OUR COMPANY; NOW IS THE TIME FOR HIM TO EARN HIS REWARD.
IF YOU MEAN YOU THINK IT IS MY JOB TO GO INTO THE SECRET PASSAGES FIRST, O THORIN THRAIN'S SON OAKENSHIELD, MAY YOUR BEARD GROW EVER LONGER, SAY SO AT ONCE AND HAVE DONE!
I MIGHT REFUSE. I HAVE GOT YOU OUT OF TWO MESSES ALREADY, SO THAT I AM, I THINK, ALREADY OWED SOME REWARD.
BUT 'THIRD TIME PAYS FOR ALL' AS MY FATHER USED TO SAY, AND SOMEHOW I DON'T THINK I SHALL REFUSE. PERHAPS I HAVE BEGUN TO TRUST MY LUCK MORE THAN I USED TO IN THE OLD DAYS, BUT ANYWAY I THINK I WILL GO AND HAVE A PEEK AT ONCE AND GET IT OVER.
NOW WHO IS COMING WITH ME?
Bilbo did not expect a chorus of volunteers, so he was not disappointed. But old Balin, the look-out man, was rather fond of the hobbit.
I WILL COME INSIDE AT LEAST AND PERHAPS A BIT OF THE WAY TOO, READY TO CALL FOR HELP IF NECESSARY.

The most that can be said for the dwarves is this; they intended to pay Bilbo really handsomely for his services; they had brought him to do a nasty job for them, and they did not mind the poor little fellow doing it if he would; but they would all have done their best to get him out of trouble, if he got into it.

There it is: dwarves are not heroes, but calculating folk with a great idea of the value of money; some are tricky and treacherous and pretty bad lots; some are not, but are decent enough people like Thorin and company, if you don't expect too much.

It was far easier going than Bilbo expected. This was no goblin entrance, or rough Wood-elves' cave. It was a passage made by dwarves, at the height of their wealth and skill.

Balin stopped where he could still see the faint outline of the door, and by a trick of the echoes of the tunnel hear the rustle of the whispering voices of the others just outside.

GOOD LUCK, MISTER BAGGINS.

Then the hobbit slipped on his ring, and warned by the echoes to take more than hobbit's care to make no sound, he crept noiselessly down, down, down into the dark. He was trembling with fear, but his little face was set and grim. Already he was a very different hobbit than the one that had run out without a pocket-handkerchief from Bag-End long ago.

NOW YOU ARE IN FOR IT AT LAST, BILBO BAGGINS.

YOU WENT AND PUT YOUR FOOT RIGHT IN IT THAT NIGHT OF THE PARTY. I HAVE ABSOLUTELY NO USE FOR DRAGON-GUARDED TREASURES, AND THE WHOLE LOT COULD STAY HERE FOR-EVER, IF ONLY I COULD WAKE UP AND FIND THIS BEASTLY TUNNEL WAS MY OWN FRONT-HALL AT HOME!

IS THAT A KIND OF A GLOW I SEEM TO SEE COMING RIGHT AHEAD DOWN THERE?

It was. As he went forward it grew and grew. Also it was now undoubtedly hot in the tunnel. A sound, too, began to throb in his ears, a sound that grew to the unmistakable gurgling noise of some vast animal snoring in its sleep down there in the red glow in front of him.

It was at this point that Bilbo stopped. Going on was the bravest thing he ever did. The tremendous things that happened afterward were as nothing compared to it. He fought the real battle in the tunnel alone, before he ever saw the vast danger that lay in wait.

At any rate after a short halt, go on he did, coming to the end of the tunnel. It was almost dark, but rising from the near side of the rocky floor there was a great glow.

The glow of Smaug!

To say that Bilbo's breath was taken away is no description at all. There are no words left to express his staggerment, since Men changed the language that they learned of elves in the days when all the world was wonderful.

Bilbo had heard tell and sing of dragon hoards before, but the splendour, the lust, the glory of such treasure had never yet come home to him.

His heart was filled and pierced with enchantment and with the desire of dwarves; and he gazed motionless, almost forgetting the frightful guardian, at the gold beyond price and count.

He gazed for what seemed an age, before drawn almost against his will, he stole across the floor to the nearest edge of the mounds of treasure. Above him the sleeping dragon lay, a dire menace even in his sleep.
He grasped a great two-handled cup, as heavy as he could carry, and cast one fearful eye upwards.
Smaug's snoring changed its note.
Then Bilbo fled. His heart was beating and a more fevered shaking was in his legs than when he was going down.
I'VE DONE IT! THIS WILL SHOW THEM. 'MORE LIKE A GROCER THAN A BURGLAR' INDEED! WELL, WE'LL HEAR NO MORE OF THAT.
Nor did he. The dwarves were overjoyed to see the hobbit again. They praised him and patted him on the back and put themselves and all their families for generations to come at his service.
The dwarves were talking delightedly of the recovery of their treasure, when suddenly a vast rumbling woke in the mountain underneath as if it was an old volcano that had made up its mind to start eruptions once again, and up the long tunnel came the dreadful echoes of a bellowing and trampling that made the ground beneath them tremble.
Smaug was still to be reckoned with. It does not do to leave a live dragon out of your calculations. And he missed his cup.
Thieves! Fire! Murder! Such a thing had not happened since first he came to the Mountain! His rage passes description — the sort of rage that is only seen when rich folk that have more than they can enjoy suddenly lose something that they have long had but have never before used or wanted.

Dragons may not have much real use for all their wealth, but they know it to an ounce as a rule, especially after long possession; and Smaug was no exception.
To hunt the whole mountain till he had caught the thief and had torn and trampled him was his one thought.

QUICK! QUICK! THE DOOR! THE TUNNEL! IT'S NO GOOD HERE.
MY COUSINS BOMBUR AND BOFUR— WE HAVE FORGOTTEN THEM, THEY ARE DOWN IN THE VALLEY! THEY WILL BE SLAIN, AND ALL OUR PONIES TOO, AND ALL OUR STORES LOST. WE CAN DO NOTHING!

NONSENSE! WE CANNOT LEAVE THEM. WHERE ARE THE ROPES? BE QUICK!

Up came Bofur, and all was safe. Up came Bombur, and still all was safe. Up came some tools and bundles of stores, and then danger was upon them.

A whirring noise was heard. A red light touched the points of standing rocks. The dragon came.

They had barely time to fly back to the tunnel, pulling and dragging in their bundles.

THAT'LL BE THE END OF OUR POOR BEASTS! NOTHING CAN ESCAPE SMAUG ONCE HE SEES IT.

His hot breath shrivelled the grass before the door and drove in through the crack they had left and scorched them as they lay hid. Through the night they could hear the roar of the flying dragon. He hunted in vain till the dawn chilled his wrath. Smaug would not forget or forgive the theft, not if a thousand years turned him to smouldering stone, but he could afford to wait. Slow and silent he crept back to his lair and half closed his eyes.

HERE WE ARE AND HERE WE SHALL HAVE TO STAY, UNLESS ANY ONE FANCIES TRAMPING THE LONG OPEN MILES BACK TO THE RIVER WITH SMAUG ON THE WATCH!

When morning came the terror of the dwarves grew less and they debated long on what was to be done.
WHAT DO YOU PROPOSE WE SHOULD DO, MISTER BAGGINS?
I HAVE NO IDEA AT THE MOMENT — IF YOU MEAN ABOUT REMOVING THE TREASURE. THAT OBVIOUSLY DEPENDS ENTIRELY ON SOME NEW TURN OF LUCK AND THE GETTING RID OF SMAUG.
GETTING RID OF DRAGONS IS NOT AT ALL IN MY LINE, BUT I WILL MAKE YOU AN OFFER. I HAVE GOT MY RING AND WILL CREEP DOWN THIS VERY NOON — THEN IF EVER SMAUG OUGHT TO BE NAPPING — AND SEE WHAT HE IS UP TO. PERHAPS SOMETHING WILL TURN UP.
'EVERY WORM HAS HIS WEAK SPOT,' AS MY FATHER USED TO SAY, THOUGH I AM SURE IT WAS NOT FROM PERSONAL EXPERIENCE.
Naturally the dwarves accepted the offer eagerly. Already they had come to respect little Bilbo. Now he had become the real leader in their adventure. He had begun to have ideas and plans of his own.
OLD SMAUG IS WEARY AND ASLEEP. HE CAN'T SEE ME AND HE WON'T HEAR ME. CHEER UP, BILBO!
He had forgotten or had never heard about dragons' sense of smell. It is also an awkward fact that they keep half an eye open watching while they sleep, if they are suspicious.
WELL, THIEF! I SMELL YOU AND I FEEL YOUR AIR. I HEAR YOUR BREATH. COME ALONG! HELP YOURSELF AGAIN, THERE IS PLENTY AND TO SPARE!
NO THANK YOU, O SMAUG THE TREMENDOUS! I DID NOT COME FOR PRESENTS. I ONLY WISHED TO HAVE A LOOK AT YOU AND SEE IF YOU WERE TRULY AS GREAT AS TALES SAY. I DID NOT BELIEVE THEM. TRULY SONGS AND TALES FALL UTTERLY SHORT OF THE REALITY.

YOU HAVE NICE MANNERS FOR A THIEF AND A LIAR.
YOU SEEM FAMILIAR WITH MY NAME, BUT I DON'T SEEM TO REMEMBER SMELLING YOU BEFORE. WHO ARE YOU AND WHERE DO YOU COME FROM, MAY I ASK?
YOU MAY INDEED! I COME FROM UNDER THE HILL, AND UNDER THE HILLS AND OVER THE HILLS MY PATHS LED. AND THROUGH THE AIR. I AM HE THAT WALKS UNSEEN. I AM RINGWINNER AND LUCKWEARER AND BARREL-RIDER!
This of course is the way to talk to dragons, if you don't want to reveal your proper name (which is wise), and don't want to infuriate them by a flat refusal (which is also very wise). No dragon can resist the fascination of riddling talk and of wasting time trying to understand it.
VERY WELL, O BARREL-RIDER! MAYBE BARREL WAS YOUR PONY'S NAME; AND MAYBE NOT. I WILL GIVE YOU ONE PIECE OF ADVICE FOR YOUR GOOD: DON'T HAVE MORE TO DO WITH DWARVES THAN YOU CAN HELP!
DWARVES!
I KNOW THE SMELL (AND TASTE) OF DWARF—NO ONE BETTER. DON'T TELL ME THAT I CAN EAT A DWARF-RIDDEN PONY AND NOT KNOW IT! I SUPPOSE YOU GOT A FAIR PRICE FOR THAT CUP LAST NIGHT?
I DON'T KNOW IF IT HAS OCCURRED TO YOU THAT EVEN IF YOU COULD STEAL THE GOLD BIT BY BIT—
A MATTER OF A HUNDRED YEARS OR SO—YOU COULD NOT GET IT VERY FAR?
Now a nasty suspicion began to grow in Bilbo's mind—had the dwarves forgotten this important point too, or were they laughing in their sleeves at him all the time?
This is the effect that dragon-talk has on the inexperienced.
I TELL YOU THAT GOLD WAS ONLY AN AFTERTHOUGHT WITH US. WE CAME OVER HILL AND UNDER HILL, BY WAVE AND WIN, FOR REVENGE!
REVENGE! REVENGE! THE KING UNDER THE MOUNTAIN IS DEAD AND WHERE ARE HIS KIN THAT DARE SEEK REVENGE? I LAID LOW THE WARRIORS OF OLD AND THEIR LIKE IS NOT IN THE WORLD TODAY.
MY ARMOUR IS LIKE TENFOLD SHIELDS, MY TEETH ARE SWORDS, MY CLAWS SPEARS, THE SHOCK OF MY TAIL A THUNDERBOLT, MY WINGS A HURRICANE, AND MY BREATH DEATH!

I HAVE ALWAYS UNDERSTOOD THAT DRAGONS WERE SOFTER UNDERNEATH, ESPECIALLY IN THE REGION OF THE— er— CHEST; BUT DOUBTLESS ONE SO FORTIFIED HAS THOUGHT OF THAT.

YOUR INFORMATION IS ANTIQUATED. LOOK!
I AM ARMOURED ABOVE AND BELOW WITH IRON SCALES AND HARD GEMS. NO BLADE CAN PIERCE ME.
WHAT DO YOU SAY TO THAT?
DAZZLINGLY MARVELLOUS! PERFECT! FLAWLESS! STAGGERING!

But what Bilbo thought inside was: "Old fool! Why, there is a large patch in the hollow of his left breast as bare as a snail out of his shell!"

WELL, I REALLY MUST NOT DETAIN YOUR MAGNIFICENCE ANY LONGER OR KEEP YOU FROM MUCH-NEEDED REST. PONIES TAKE SOME CATCHING. AND SO DO BURGLARS!

FROOOSHH

NEVER LAUGH AT LIVE DRAGONS, BILBO YOU FOOL! YOU AREN'T NEARLY THROUGH THIS ADVENTURE YET!

The afternoon was turning to evening when he came out again. But the hobbit was worried and uncomfortable, and they had difficulty in getting anything out of him.

DRAT THE BIRD! I BELIEVE HE IS LISTENING, AND I DON'T LIKE THE LOOK OF HIM.

LEAVE HIM ALONE! THE THRUSHES ARE GOOD AND FRIENDLY. THE ANCIENT BREED THAT USED TO LIVE ABOUT HERE WERE A LONG-LIVED AND MAGICAL RACE. THE MEN OF DALE USED TO HAVE THE TRICK OF UNDERSTANDING THEIR LANGUAGE, AND USED THEM FOR MESSENGERS.

WELL, HE'LL HAVE NEWS TO TAKE TO LAKE-TOWN ALL RIGHT, IF THAT IS WHAT HE IS AFTER, THOUGH I DON'T SUPPOSE THERE ARE ANY PEOPLE LEFT THERE THAT TROUBLE WITH THRUSH-LANGUAGE.

WHY, WHAT HAS HAPPENED?

So Bilbo told them all he could remember.

I AM SURE HE KNOWS WE CAME FROM LAKE-TOWN AND HAD HELP FROM THERE; AND I HAVE A HORRIBLE FEELING THAT HIS NEXT MOVE MAY BE IN THAT DIRECTION.
I THINK YOU DID VERY WELL, IF YOU ASK ME— YOU FOUND OUT ONE VERY USEFUL THING AT ANY RATE, AND GOT HOME ALIVE. IT MAY BE A MERCY AND A BLESSING YET TO KNOW OF THE BARE PATCH IN THE OLD WORM'S DIAMOND WAISTCOAT.

All the while they talked the thrush listened, till at last when the stars began to peep forth, it silently spread its wings and flew away. And all the while they talked Bilbo became more unhappy and his foreboding grew.

I AM SURE WE ARE VERY UNSAFE HERE. SMAUG WILL BE COMING OUT ANY MINUTE NOW, AND OUR ONLY HOPE IS TO GET WELL IN THE TUNNEL AND SHUT THE DOOR.

He seemed so much in earnest that the dwarves at last did as he said, though they delayed shutting the door— it seemed a desperate plan, for no one knew whether or how they could get it open again from the inside.

And the thought of being shut in a place from which the only way out led through the dragon's lair was not one they liked.

For a long while they sat inside not far down from the half-open door and went on talking.

The talk turned to the dragon's wicked words about the dwarves. But Thorin said: "As for your share, Mister Baggins, I assure you we are more than grateful, and you shall choose your own fourteenth, as soon as we have anything to divide -- and we will do whatever we can for you, and take our share of the cost of transport when the time comes."

From that the talk turned to the great hoard itself, the great golden cup of Thror, the necklace of Girion, Lord of Dale, made of five hundred emeralds. But fairest of all was the great white gem which the dwarves had found beneath the roots of the Mountain, the heart of the Mountain, the Arkenstone of Thrain.

THE ARKENSTONE! THE ARKENSTONE! IT WAS LIKE A GLOBE WITH A THOUSAND FACETS; IT SHONE LIKE SILVER IN THE FIRELIGHT, LIKE WATER IN THE SUN, LIKE SNOW UNDER THE STARS, LIKE RAIN UPON THE MOON!

SHUT THE DOOR! I FEAR THAT DRAGON IN MY MARROW. SHUT THE DOOR BEFORE IT IS TOO LATE.

They thrust upon the door, and it closed with a snap and a clang. No trace of a keyhole was there left on the inside. They were shut in the Mountain!

And not a moment too soon.

THOOM

This was the outburst of Smaug's wrath when he could find nobody and see nothing, even where he guessed the outlet must actually be.
BARREL-RIDER! I DON'T KNOW YOUR SMELL, BUT IF YOU ARE NOT ONE OF THOSE MEN OF THE LAKE, YOU HAD THEIR HELP.

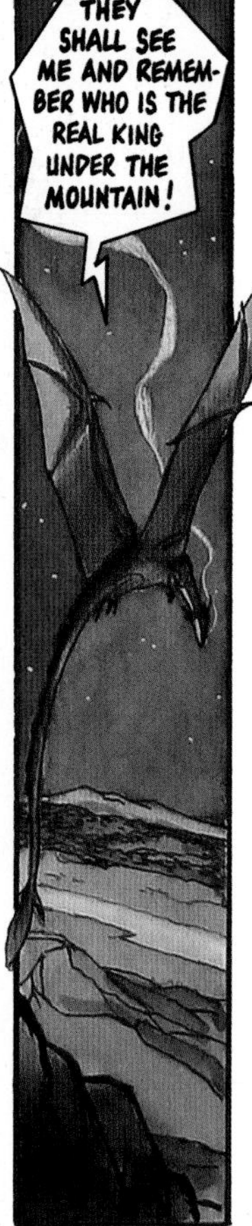

THEY SHALL SEE ME AND REMEMBER WHO IS THE REAL KING UNDER THE MOUNTAIN!

In the meanwhile, the dwarves sat in darkness. They could not count the passing time; and they scarcely dared to move. At last after days and days of waiting, as it seemed, when they were becoming choked and dazed for want of air, they could bear it no longer.
LET US TRY THE DOOR! I MUST FEEL THE WIND ON MY FACE SOON OR DIE.
I THINK I WOULD RATHER BE SMASHED BY SMAUG IN THE OPEN THAN SUFFOCATE IN HERE!

But they found that neither key nor the magic it had once obeyed would ever open that door again.
WE ARE TRAPPED! THIS IS THE END. WE SHALL DIE HERE!
COME, COME! 'WHILE THERE'S LIFE THERE'S HOPE!' AS MY FATHER USED TO SAY, AND 'THIRD TIME PAYS FOR ALL.' I AM GOING DOWN THE TUNNEL ONCE AGAIN. THE ONLY WAY OUT IS DOWN. AND I THINK THIS TIME YOU HAD BETTER ALL COME WITH ME.

In desperation they ageeed. Down, down they went, but though every now and again Bilbo in fear stopped and listened, not a sound stirred below.

NOW I WONDER WHAT ON EARTH SMAUG IS PLAYING AT.
PERHAPS WE CAN MAKE A LITTLE LIGHT, AND HAVE A LOOK ROUND BEFORE THE LUCK TURNS.
But Bilbo could not persuade the dwarves to join him, for as Thorin carefully explained, Mister Baggins was still officially their expert burglar and investigator. If he liked to risk light, that was his affair. They would wait in the tunnel for his report.

So they sat near the door and watched. Every now and again, while he was still near enough, they caught a glint and a tinkle as he stumbled on some golden thing.
Then they sam him halt and stoop for a moment; but they did not know the reason.

It was the Arkenstone, the Heart of the Mountain. So Bilbo guessed from Thorin's description; but indeed there could not be two such gems, even in so marvellous a hoard, even in all the world.

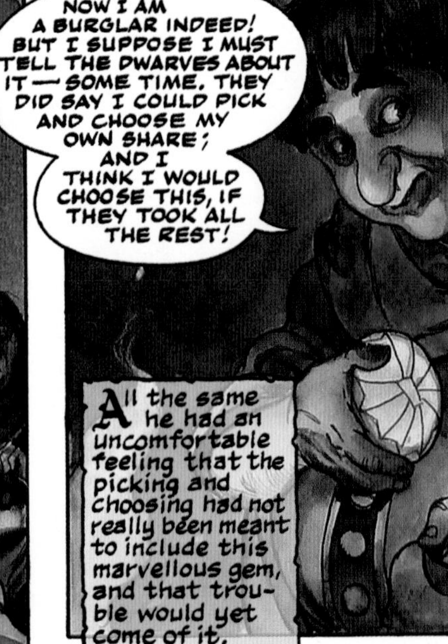
NOW I AM A BURGLAR INDEED! BUT I SUPPOSE I MUST TELL THE DWARVES ABOUT IT — SOME TIME. THEY DID SAY I COULD PICK AND CHOOSE MY OWN SHARE; AND I THINK I WOULD CHOOSE THIS, IF THEY TOOK ALL THE REST!
All the same he had an uncomfortable feeling that the picking and choosing had not really been meant to include this marvellous gem, and that trouble would yet come of it.

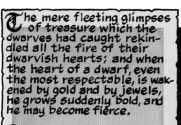

The mere fleeting glimpses of treasure which the dwarves had caught rekindled all the fire of their dwarvish hearts; and when the heart of a dwarf, even the most respectable, is wakened by gold and by jewels, he grows suddenly bold, and he may become fierce.

The dwarves indeed no longer needed any urging. All were now eager to explore the hall while they had the chance, and willing to believe that, for the present, Smaug was away from home.

They gathered gems and stuffed their pockets, and let what they could not carry fall back through their fingers with a sigh. Thorin was not least among these, but always he searched from side to side for something which he could not find. It was the Arkenstone; but he spoke of it yet to no one.

Now the dwarves took down mail and weapons from the walls, and armed themselves.

MISTER BAGGINS! HERE IS THE FIRST PAYMENT OF YOUR REWARD! CAST OFF YOUR OLD COAT AND PUT ON THIS!
I FEEL MAGNIFICENT, BUT I EXPECT I LOOK RATHER ABSURD. HOW THEY WOULD LAUGH ON THE HILL AT HOME! STILL I WISH THERE WAS A LOOKING-GLASS HANDY!

THORIN! WHAT NEXT? WE ARE ARMED, BUT WHAT GOOD HAS ANY ARMOUR EVER BEEN BEFORE AGAINST SMAUG THE DREADFUL? THIS TREASURE IS NOT YET WON BACK. WE ARE NOT LOOKING FOR GOLD YET, BUT FOR A WAY OF ESCAPE; AND WE HAVE TEMPTED LUCK TOO LONG!

YOU SPEAK THE TRUTH! LET US GO! I WILL GUIDE YOU. NOT IN A THOUSAND YEARS SHOULD I FORGET THE WAYS OF THE PALACE.

They climbed long stairs, and turned and went down wide echoing ways, and turned again and climbed yet more stairs, and yet more stairs-

—and behold! Before them stood the bright light of day!

WELL! I NEVER EXPECTED TO BE LOOKING *OUT* OF THIS DOOR, AND I NEVER EXPECTED TO BE SO PLEASED TO SEE THE SUN AGAIN, AND TO FEEL THE WIND ON MY FACE, BUT—OW! THIS WIND IS COLD! AND I DON'T FEEL THAT SMAUG'S FRONT DOORSTEP IS THE SAFEST PLACE—
DO LET'S GO SOMEWHERE WHERE WE CAN SIT QUIET FOR A BIT!

QUITE RIGHT! AND I THINK I KNOW WHICH WAY WE SHOULD GO: WE OUGHT TO MAKE FOR THE OLD LOOK-OUT POST AT THE SOUTH-WEST CORNER OF THE MOUNTAIN.
HOW FAR IS THAT?
ABOUT FIVE HOURS MARCH, I SHOULD THINK. THERE IS (OR WAS) A PATH THAT LEFT THE ROAD AND CLIMBED UP TO THE POST ON RAVENHILL, A HARD CLIMB, TOO, EVEN IF THE OLD STEPS ARE STILL THERE.

DEAR ME! MORE WALKING AND MORE CLIMBING WITHOUT BREAKFAST! I WONDER HOW MANY BREAKFASTS AND OTHER MEALS WE HAVE MISSED INSIDE THAT NASTY CLOCKLESS, TIMELESS HOLE?

As a matter of fact two nights and the day between had gone by (and not altogether without food) since the dragon smashed the magic door, but Bilbo had quite lost count, and it might have been one night or a week of nights for all he could tell.

COME, COME! DON'T CALL MY PLACE A NASTY HOLE! YOU WAIT TILL IT HAS BEEN CLEANED AND REDECORATED!
THAT WON'T BE TILL SMAUG'S DEAD. IN THE MEANWHILE WHERE IS HE? I WOULD GIVE A GOOD BREAKFAST TO KNOW. I HOPE HE IS NOT UP ON THE MOUNTAIN LOOKING DOWN AT US!

After going a short way they rested for a while and had such a breakfast as they could, chiefly *cram* and water. (If you want to know what *cram* is, I can only say that I don't know the recipe; but it is biscuitish, keeps good indefinitely, is supposed to be sustaining, and is certainly not entertaining, being in fact very uninteresting except as a chewing exercise. It was made by the Lake-men for long journeys.)
After that they went on again till at last in the late afternoon they came to the top of the ridge and saw the wintry sun going downwards to the West.
HERE IN THE OLD DAYS WE USED ALWAYS TO KEEP WATCHMEN. THE GUARDS WERE MADE OVER COMFORTABLE PERHAPS—OTHERWISE WE MIGHT HAVE HAD LONGER WARNINGS OF THE COMING OF THE DRAGON, AND THINGS MIGHT HAVE BEEN DIFFERENT. STILL, HERE WE CAN NOW LIE HID AND SHELTERED FOR A WHILE, AND CAN SEE MUCH WITHOUT BEING SEEN.
NOT MUCH USE, IF WE HAVE BEEN SEEN COMING HERE.
From the rock-chamber they looked West and there was nothing, and East there was nothing, and in the South there was no sign of the dragon, but there was a gathering of very many birds. At that they gazed and wondered; but they were no nearer understanding it, when the first cold stars came out.
Now if you wish, like the dwarves, to hear news of Smaug, you must go back again to the evening when he smashed the door and flew off in a rage, two days before.
LOOK! THE LIGHTS AGAIN! LAST NIGHT THE WATCHMEN SAW THEM START AND FADE FROM MIDNIGHT UNTIL DAWN. SOMETHING IS HAPPENING UP THERE.
PERHAPS THE KING UNDER THE MOUNTAIN IS FORGING GOLD. IT IS LONG SINCE HE WENT NORTH. IT IS TIME THE SONGS BEGAN TO PROVE THEMSELVES AGAIN.
WHICH KING? AS LIKE AS NOT IT IS THE MARAUDING FIRE OF THE DRAGON, THE ONLY KING UNDER THE MOUNTAIN WE HAVE EVER KNOWN.
YOU ARE ALWAYS FOREBODING GLOOMY THINGS! ANYTHING FROM FLOODS TO POISONED FISH. THINK OF SOMETHING CHEERFUL!
THE RIVER IS RUNNING GOLD FROM THE MOUNTAIN!
THE DRAGON IS COMING OR I AM A FOOL! CUT THE BRIDGES! TO ARMS! TO ARMS!
Then warning trumpets were suddenly sounded, and echoed along the rocky shores. Every vessel in the town was filled with water, every warrior was armed, every arrow and dart was ready, and the bridge to the land was thrown down and destroyed.
So it was that the dragon did not find them quite unprepared.

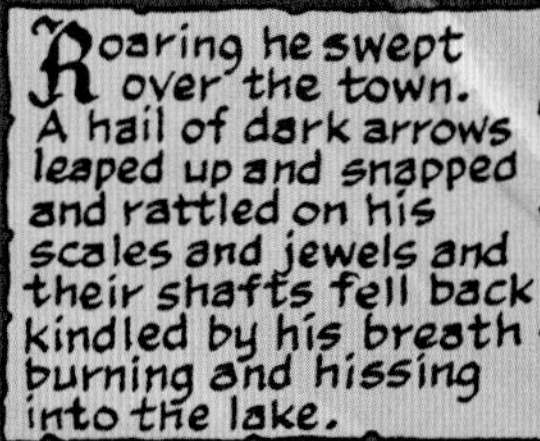
Roaring he swept over the town. A hail of dark arrows leaped up and snapped and rattled on his scales and jewels and their shafts fell back kindled by his breath burning and hissing into the lake.
At the twanging of the bows and the shrilling of the trumpets the dragon's wrath blazed to its height, till he was blind and mad with it.
Amid shrieks and wailing and the shouts of men Smaug came over them, swept towards the bridges and was foiled! The bridge was gone, and his enemies were on an island in deep water-too deep and dark and cool for his liking.
No one had dared to give battle to him for many an age; nor would they have dared now, if it had not been for the grim-voiced man (Bard was his name), who ran to and fro cheering on the archers and urging the Master to order them to fight to the last arrow.

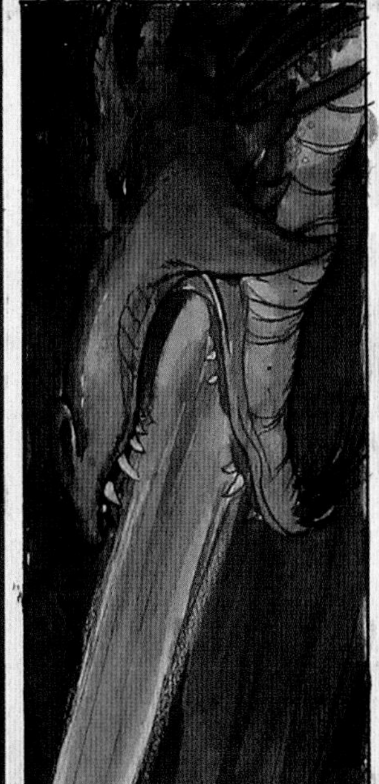
Fire leaped from the dragon's jaws. Down he swooped straight through the arrow-storm, reckless in his rage, taking no heed to turn his scaly sides towards his foes, seeking only to set their town ablaze.

THOOOM
Flames unquenchable sprang high into the night. Another swoop and another, and another house and then another sprang afire and fell; and still no arrow hindered Smaug or hurt him more than a fly from the marshes.

Already men were jumping into the water on every side. Women and children were being huddled into laden boats in the market-pool. The Master himself was turning to his great gilded boat, hoping to row away in the confusion and save himself.
Soon all the town would be deserted and burned down to the surface of the lake.

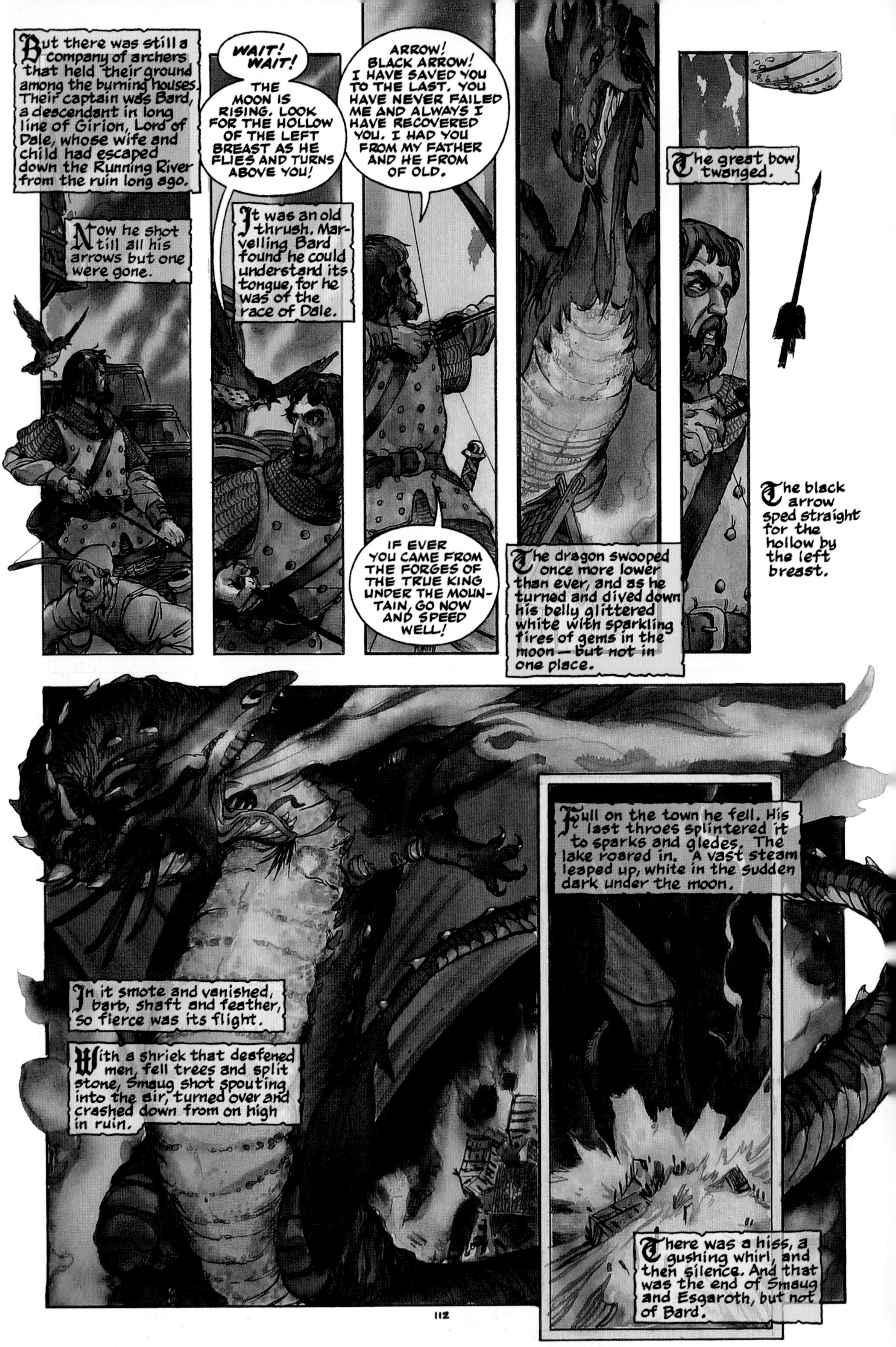

But there was still a company of archers that held their ground among the burning houses. Their captain was Bard, a descendant in long line of Girion, Lord of Dale, whose wife and child had escaped down the Running River from the ruin long ago.

Now he shot till all his arrows but one were gone.

WAIT! WAIT!

THE MOON IS RISING. LOOK FOR THE HOLLOW OF THE LEFT BREAST AS HE FLIES AND TURNS ABOVE YOU!

It was an old thrush. Marvelling Bard found he could understand its tongue, for he was of the race of Dale.

ARROW! BLACK ARROW! I HAVE SAVED YOU TO THE LAST. YOU HAVE NEVER FAILED ME AND ALWAYS I HAVE RECOVERED YOU. I HAD YOU FROM MY FATHER AND HE FROM OF OLD.

IF EVER YOU CAME FROM THE FORGES OF THE TRUE KING UNDER THE MOUNTAIN, GO NOW AND SPEED WELL!

The dragon swooped once more lower than ever, and as he turned and dived down his belly glittered white with sparkling fires of gems in the moon — but not in one place.

The great bow twanged.

The black arrow sped straight for the hollow by the left breast.

In it smote and vanished, barb, shaft and feather, so fierce was its flight.

With a shriek that deafened men, fell trees and split stone, Smaug shot spouting into the air, turned over and crashed down from on high in ruin.

Full on the town he fell. His last throes splintered it to sparks and gledes. The lake roared in. A vast steam leaped up, white in the sudden dark under the moon.

There was a hiss, a gushing whirl, and then silence. And that was the end of Smaug and Esgaroth, but not of Bard.

Down the wind came the voices of the people of Esgaroth lamenting their lost town and goods and ruined houses, and their first complaints and anger were against the Master, who had left the town so soon, while some were still willing to defend it.
HE MAY HAVE A GOOD HEAD FOR BUSINESS — ESPECIALLY HIS OWN BUSINESS, BUT HE IS NO GOOD WHEN ANYTHING SERIOUS HAPPENS!
IF ONLY BARD HAD NOT BEEN KILLED, WE WOULD MAKE HIM A KING. BARD THE DRAGON-SHOOTER OF THE LINE OF GIRION! ALAS HE IS LOST!
BARD IS NOT LOST! HE DIVED FROM ESGAROTH, WHEN THE ENEMY WAS SLAIN. I AM BARD, OF THE LINE OF GIRION; I AM THE SLAYER OF THE DRAGON.
KING BARD!
KING BARD!
GIRION WAS LORD OF DALE, NOT KING OF ESGAROTH. IN THE LAKE-TOWN WE HAVE ALWAYS ELECTED MASTERS FROM AMONG THE OLD AND WISE, AND HAVE NOT ENDURED THE RULE OF MERE FIGHTING MEN.
LET 'KING BARD' GO BACK TO HIS OWN KINGDOM — DALE IS NOW FREED BY HIS VALOUR, AND NOTHING HINDERS HIS RETURN. AND ANY THAT WISH CAN GO WITH HIM. THE WISE WILL STAY HERE AND HOPE TO REBUILD OUR TOWN.
UP THE BOWMAN, AND DOWN WITH MONEY-BAGS!
I AM THE LAST MAN TO UNDER-VALUE BARD THE BOWMAN. BUT, WHY O PEOPLE? WHY DO I GET ALL YOUR BLAME? WHO AROUSED THE DRAGON FROM HIS SLUMBER, I MIGHT ASK? WHO OBTAINED OF US RICH GIFTS AND AMPLE HELP, AND LED US TO BELIEVE THAT OLD SONGS COULD COME TRUE? WHAT SORT OF GOLD HAVE THEY SENT DOWN THE RIVER TO REWARD US?
DRAGON-FIRE AND RUIN! FROM WHOM SHOULD WE CLAIM THE RECOMPENSE OF OUR DAMAGE, AND AID FOR OUR WIDOWS AND ORPHANS?
WHY WASTE WORDS AND WRATH ON THOSE UNHAPPY CREATURES? DOUBTLESS THEY PERISHED FIRST IN FIRE, BEFORE SMAUG CAME TO US.
Then even as he was speaking, the thought came into his heart of the fabled treasure of the Mountain lying without guard or owner. He thought of the Master's words, and of Dale rebuilt and filled with golden bells, if he could but find the men.
THIS IS NO TIME FOR ANGRY WORDS, MASTER, OR FOR CONSIDERING WEIGHTY PLANS OF CHANGE. THERE IS WORK TO DO. I SERVE YOU STILL — THOUGH AFTER A WHILE I MAY THINK AGAIN OF YOUR WORDS AND GO NORTH WITH ANY THAT WILL FOLLOW ME.

Bard strode off to help in the ordering of the camps and in the care of the sick and the wounded. And everywhere he went he found talk running like fire among the people concerning the vast treasure that was now unguarded; and it cheered them greatly in their plight.

That was well, for the night was bitter and miserable. Shelters could be contrived for few (the Master had one) and there was little food (even the Master went short). Many took ill of wet and cold and sorrow that night, and afterwards died.

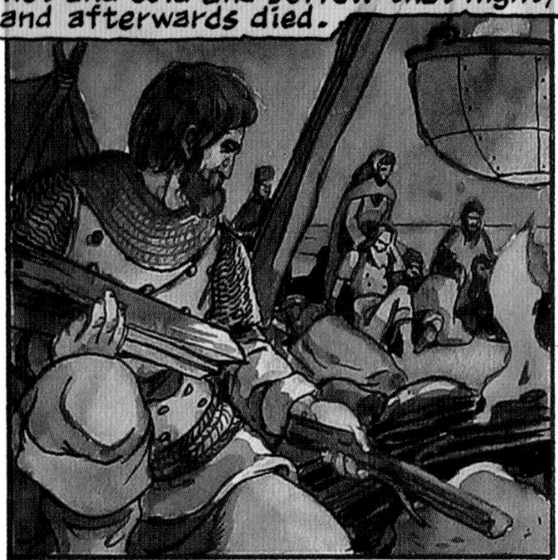

In the days that followed there was much sickness and great hunger.

Meanwhile Bard took the lead, and ordered things as he wished, though always in the Master's name. Probably most of the people would have perished in the winter that now hurried after autumn, if help had not been to hand.

But help came swiftly; for Bard at once had speedy messengers sent up the river to the Forest to ask the aid of the King of the Elves of the Wood, and those messengers had found a host already on the move, although it was then only the third day after the fall of Smaug.

The Elvenking had received news from his own messengers and from the birds that loved his folk, and already knew much of what had happened. Very great indeed was the commotion among all things with wings that dwelt on the borders of the Desolation of the Dragon.

Far over Mirkwood tidings spread: "Smaug is dead!" Even before the Elvenking rode forth, the news had passed west right to the pinewoods of the Misty Mountains; Beorn had heard it in his wooden house, and the goblins were at council in their caves.

But the king, when he received the prayers of Bard, had pity; so turning his march, which had at first been direct towards the Mountain—for he too had not forgotten the legend of the wealth of Thror—he hastened now down the river to the Long Lake. He had not boats or rafts enough for his host, but great store of goods he sent ahead by water.

Only five days after the death of the dragon they came upon the shores and looked on the ruins of the town. The Master was ready to make any bargain for the future in return for the Elvenking's aid.

Their plans were soon made. The Master remained behind, and with him were some men of crafts and many skilled elves; and they busied themselves felling trees, and raising huts by the shore against the oncoming winter.

But all the men of arms who were still able, and the most of the Elvenking's array, got ready to march north to the Mountain. It was thus that in eleven days from the ruin of the town the head of their host passed the rock-gates at the end of the lake and came into the desolate lands.

Before long there was a fluttering of wings, and back came the thrush; and with him came a most decrepit old bird.

O THORIN SON OF THRAIN, AND BALIN SON OF FUNDIN, I AM ROÄC SON OF CARC. CARC IS DEAD, BUT HE WAS WELL KNOWN TO YOU ONCE. NOW I AM THE CHIEF OF THE GREAT RAVENS OF THE MOUNTAIN.

BEHOLD! THE BIRDS ARE GATHERING BACK AGAIN TO THE MOUNTAIN AND TO DALE FROM SOUTH AND EAST AND WEST, FOR WORD HAS GONE OUT THAT SMAUG IS DEAD!

BUT MANY ARE GATHERING HERE BESIDE THE BIRDS. ALREADY A HOST OF THE ELVES IS ON THE WAY, AND CARRION BIRDS ARE WITH THEM HOPING FOR BATTLE AND SLAUGHTER.

BY THE LAKE MEN MURMUR THAT THEIR SORROWS ARE DUE TO THE DWARVES; FOR THEY ARE HOMELESS AND MANY HAVE DIED, AND SMAUG HAS DESTROYED THEIR TOWN. THEY TOO THINK TO FIND AMENDS FROM YOUR TREASURE, WHETHER YOU ARE ALIVE OR DEAD.

THIRTEEN IS A SMALL REMNANT OF THE GREAT FOLK OF DURIN THAT ONCE DWELT HERE. IF YOU WILL LISTEN TO MY COUNSEL, YOU WILL NOT TRUST THE MASTER OF THE LAKE-MEN, BUT RATHER HIM THAT SHOT THE DRAGON WITH HIS BOW.

WE WOULD SEE PEACE ONCE MORE AMONG DWARVES AND MEN AND ELVES AFTER THE LONG DESOLATION; BUT IT MAY COST YOU DEAR IN GOLD. I HAVE SPOKEN.

OUR THANKS, ROÄC CARC'S SON, YOU AND YOUR PEOPLE SHALL NOT BE FORGOTTEN. BUT NONE OF OUR GOLD SHALL THIEVES TAKE OR THE VIOLENT CARRY OFF WHILE WE ARE ALIVE.
ALSO I WOULD BEG OF YOU, THAT YOU WOULD SEND MESSENGERS TO MY COUSIN DAIN IN THE IRON HILLS, FOR HE HAS MANY PEOPLE WELL-ARMED AND DWELLS NEAREST TO THIS PLACE. BID HIM HASTEN!

I WILL NOT SAY IF THIS COUNSEL BE GOOD OR BAD, BUT I WILL DO WHAT CAN BE DONE.
BACK NOW TO THE MOUNTAIN! WE HAVE LITTLE TIME TO LOSE!

As you have heard some of the events already, you will see that the dwarves still had some days before them. So now they began to labour hard in fortifying the main entrance. Tools were to be found in plenty; and at such work the dwarves were still very skilled.

As they worked the ravens brought them constant tidings. In this way they learned that the Elvenking had turned aside to the lake, and they still had a breathing space.

In four days time they knew that the joined armies of the Lake-men and the Elves were hurrying towards the Mountain. But now their hopes were higher; for they had food for some weeks with care—chiefly *cram*, of course, and they were very tired of it; but *cram* is much better than nothing—and already the gate was blocked with a wall of squared stones laid dry, but very thick and high across the opening.

There came a night when suddenly there were many lights as of fires and torches away south in Dale before them.
THEY HAVE COME! AND THEIR CAMP IS VERY GREAT. THEY MUST HAVE COME INTO THE VALLEY UNDER THE COVER OF DUSK ALONG BOTH BANKS OF THE RIVER.
That night the dwarves slept little.

The morning was still pale when they saw a company approaching. Before long they could see that both men of the lake armed as if for war and elvish bowmen were among them.

WHO ARE YOU THAT COME ARMED AS IF IN WAR TO THE GATES OF THORIN SON OF THRAIN, KING UNDER THE MOUNTAIN, AND WHAT DO YOU DESIRE?

HAIL, THORIN! WE REJOICE THAT YOU ARE ALIVE BEYOND OUR HOPE. I AM BARD, AND BY MY HAND WAS THE DRAGON SLAIN AND YOUR TREASURE DELIVERED.

MOREOVER I AM BY RIGHT DESCENT THE HEIR OF GIRION OF DALE, AND IN YOUR HOARD IS MINGLED MUCH OF THE WEALTH OF HIS HALLS AND TOWN, WHICH OF OLD SMAUG STOLE. IS NOT THAT A MATTER OF WHICH WE MAY SPEAK?

FURTHER, IN HIS LAST BATTLE SMAUG DESTROYED THE DWELLINGS OF THE MEN OF ESGAROTH, AND I AM YET THE SERVANT OF THEIR MASTER. I WOULD SPEAK FOR HIM AND ASK WHETHER YOU HAVE NO THOUGHT FOR THE SORROW AND MISERY OF HIS PEOPLE. THEY AIDED YOU IN YOUR DISTRESS, AND IN RECOMPENSE YOU HAVE THUS FAR BROUGHT RUIN ONLY, THOUGH DOUBTLESS UNDESIGNED.

Now these were fair words and true, if proudly and grimly spoken; and Bilbo thought that Thorin would at once admit what justice was in them. But he did not reckon with the power that gold has upon which a dragon has long brooded, nor with dwarvish hearts.
TO THE TREASURE OF MY PEOPLE NO MAN HAS A CLAIM, BECAUSE SMAUG WHO STOLE IT FROM US ALSO ROBBED HIM OF LIFE OR HOME. THE GOLD WAS NOT HIS THAT HIS EVIL DEEDS SHOULD BE AMENDED WITH A SHARE OF IT. THE PRICE OF THE GOODS AND THE ASSISTANCE THAT WE RECEIVED OF THE LAKE-MEN WE WILL FAIRLY PAY— IN DUE TIME.
BUT NOTHING WILL WE GIVE, NOT EVEN A LOAF'S WORTH, UNDER THREAT OF FORCE. NOR WILL I PARLEY WITH THE PEOPLE OF THE ELVENKING, WHOM I REMEMBER WITH SMALL KINDNESS. IN THIS DEBATE THEY HAVE NO PLACE. BE GONE NOW ERE OUR ARROWS FLY!

THE ELVENKING IS MY FRIEND, AND HE HAS SUCCOURED THE PEOPLE OF THE LAKE IN THEIR NEED, THOUGH THEY HAD NO CLAIM BUT FRIENDSHIP ON HIM.

WE WILL GIVE YOU TIME TO REPENT YOUR WORDS. GATHER YOUR WISDOM ERE WE RETURN.

Ere many hours were past, the banner-bearers returned, and trumpeters stood forth and blew a blast:
IN THE NAME OF ESGAROTH AND THE FOREST WE SPEAK UNTO THORIN THRAIN'S SON OAKENSHIELD, AND WE BID HIM CONSIDER WELL THE CLAIMS THAT HAVE BEEN URGED, OR BE DECLARED OUR FOE.
AT THE LEAST HE SHALL DELIVER ONE TWELFTH PORTION OF THE TREASURE UNTO BARD, AS THE DRAGON-SLAYER, AND AS THE HEIR OF GIRION. FROM THAT PORTION BARD WILL HIMSELF CONTRIBUTE TO THE AID OF ESGAROTH.

BUT IF THORIN WOULD HAVE THE FRIENDSHIP AND HONOUR OF THE LANDS ABOUT, AS HIS SIRES HAD OF OLD, THEN HE WILL GIVE ALSO SOMEWHAT OF HIS OWN FOR THE COMFORT OF THE MEN OF THE LAKE.

THAK
SINCE SUCH IS YOUR ANSWER, I DECLARE THE MOUNTAIN BESIEGED. YOU SHALL NOT DEPART FROM IT, UNTIL YOU CALL ON YOUR SIDE FOR A TRUCE AND A PARLEY. WE WILL BEAR NO WEAPONS AGAINST YOU, BUT WE LEAVE YOU TO YOUR GOLD. YOU MAY EAT THAT, IF YOU WILL!

The days passed slowly and wearily. So grim had Thorin become, that even if they had wished, the others would not have dared to find fault with him; but indeed most of them seemed to share his mind—except perhaps old fat Bombur and Fili and Kili. Bilbo of course disapproved of the whole turn of affairs.
THE WHOLE PLACE STILL STINKS OF DRAGON AND IT MAKES ME SICK. AND CRAM IS BEGINNING SIMPLY TO STICK IN MY THROAT.

SEARCH EVERY CORNER. FOR THE ARKENSTONE OF MY FATHER IS WORTH MORE THAN A RIVER OF GOLD IN ITSELF, AND TO ME IT IS BEYOND PRICE. THAT STONE OF ALL THE TREASURE I NAME UNTO MYSELF, AND I WILL BE AVENGED ON ANYONE WHO FINDS IT AND WITHHOLDS IT.
All the same Bilbo did not speak of it, for as the weariness of the days grew heavier, the beginnings of a plan had come into his little head.

Then the ravens brought news that Dain and more than five hundred dwarves were now within about two days' march of Dale.
THOUGH THEY ARE A GRIM FOLK, THEY ARE NOT LIKELY TO OVERCOME THE HOST THAT BESETS YOU; AND EVEN IF THEY DID SO, WHAT WILL YOU GAIN? WINTER AND SNOW IS HASTENING BEHIND THEM. HOW SHALL YOU BE FED WITHOUT THE FRIENDSHIP AND GOOD-WILL OF THE LANDS ABOUT YOU? THE TREASURE IS LIKELY TO BE YOUR DEATH, THOUGH THE DRAGON IS NO MORE!
WINTER AND SNOW WILL BITE BOTH MEN AND ELVES. WITH MY FRIENDS BEHIND THEM AND WINTER UPON THEM, THEY WILL PERHAPS BE IN SOFTER MOOD TO PARLEY WITH.

That night Bilbo made up his mind.

IT IS MIGHTY COLD! I WISH WE COULD HAVE A FIRE UP HERE AS THEY HAVE IN THE CAMP!

IT IS WARM ENOUGH INSIDE. IT IS LONG SINCE I WATCHED, AND I WILL TAKE YOUR TURN FOR YOU, IF YOU LIKE. THERE IS NO SLEEP IN ME TONIGHT.

YOU ARE A GOOD FELLOW, MISTER BAGGINS, AND I WILL TAKE YOUR OFFER KINDLY. IF THERE SHOULD BE ANYTHING TO NOTE, ROUSE ME FIRST, MIND YOU!

OFF YOU GO! I WILL WAKE YOU AT MIDNIGHT, AND YOU CAN WAKE THE NEXT WATCHMAN.

As soon as Bombur had gone, Bilbo put on his ring, slipped down over the wall, and was gone. He had about five hours before him. Bombur would sleep and all the others were busy with Thorin.

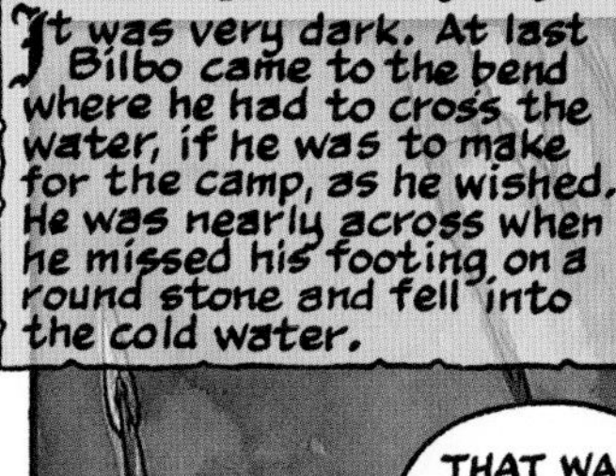

It was very dark. At last Bilbo came to the bend where he had to cross the water, if he was to make for the camp, as he wished. He was nearly across when he missed his footing on a round stone and fell into the cold water.

THAT WAS NO FISH! THERE IS A SPY ABOUT. HIDE YOUR LIGHTS!
THEY WILL HELP HIM MORE THAN US, IF IT IS THAT QUEER LITTLE CREATURE THAT IS SAID TO BE THEIR SERVANT.

SERVANT INDEED! LET'S HAVE A LIGHT! I AM HERE, IF YOU WANT ME!
WHO ARE YOU? ARE YOU THE DWARVES' HOBBIT? WHAT ARE YOU DOING?

I AM MISTER BILBO BAGGINS, COMPANION OF THORIN IF YOU WANT TO KNOW. I KNOW YOUR KING WELL BY SIGHT, THOUGH PERHAPS HE DOESN'T KNOW ME TO LOOK AT ME. BUT BARD WILL REMEMBER ME. AND IT IS BARD I PARTICULARLY WANT TO SEE.
IF YOU WISH EVER TO GET BACK TO YOUR OWN WOODS FROM THIS COLD CHEERLESS PLACE YOU WILL LET ME SPEAK TO YOUR CHIEFS AS QUICK AS MAY BE. I HAVE ONLY AN HOUR OR TWO TO SPARE.

REALLY YOU KNOW THINGS ARE IMPOSSIBLE. PERSONALLY I AM TIRED OF THE WHOLE AFFAIR.
BUT I HAVE AN INTEREST IN THIS MATTER—ONE FOURTEENTH SHARE TO BE PRECISE, ACCORDING TO A LETTER, WHICH FORTUNATELY I HAVE KEPT.
A SHARE OF THE *PROFITS*, MIND YOU. PERSONALLY I AM ONLY TOO READY TO CONSIDER ALL YOUR CLAIMS CAREFULLY, AND DEDUCT WHAT IS RIGHT FROM THE TOTAL BEFORE PUTTING IN MY OWN CLAIM.
HOWEVER YOU DON'T KNOW THORIN OAKENSHIELD AS WELL AS I DO NOW. I ASSURE YOU, HE IS QUITE READY TO SIT ON A HEAP OF GOLD AND STARVE, AS LONG AS YOU SIT HERE.
AT THE SAME TIME WINTER IS COMING ON FAST. ALSO THERE WILL BE OTHER DIFFICULTIES. DAIN OF THE IRON HILLS, I MAY TELL YOU, IS NOW LESS THAN TWO DAYS' MARCH OFF, AND HAS AT LEAST FIVE HUNDRED GRIM DWARVES WITH HIM. WHEN THEY ARRIVE THERE MAY BE SERIOUS TROUBLE.
WHY DO YOU TELL US THIS? ARE YOU BETRAYING YOUR FRIENDS, OR ARE YOU THREATENING US?
MY DEAR BARD! DON'T BE SO HASTY. I AM MERELY TRYING TO AVOID TROUBLES FOR ALL CONCERNED. NOW I WILL MAKE YOU AN OFFER!
IT IS THIS!
THIS IS THE ARKENSTONE OF THRAIN, THE HEART OF THE MOUNTAIN, AND IT IS ALSO THE HEART OF THORIN. HE VALUES IT ABOVE A RIVER OF GOLD. I GIVE IT TO YOU. IT WILL AID YOU IN YOUR BARGAINING.
BUT HOW IS IT YOURS TO GIVE?
O WELL! IT ISN'T EXACTLY; BUT, WELL, I AM WILLING TO LET IT STAND AGAINST ALL MY CLAIM, DON'T YOU KNOW. I MAY BE A BURGLAR—BUT I AM AN HONEST ONE, I HOPE, MORE OR LESS. ANYWAY I AM GOING BACK NOW, AND THE DWARVES CAN DO WHAT THEY LIKE TO ME.
BILBO BAGGINS! YOU ARE MORE WORTHY TO WEAR THE ARMOUR OF ELF-PRINCES THAN MANY THAT HAVE LOOKED MORE COMELY IN IT. BUT I WONDER IF THORIN OAKENSHIELD WILL SEE IT SO. I ADVISE YOU TO REMAIN WITH US, AND HERE YOU SHALL BE HONOURED AND THRICE WELCOME.
THANK YOU VERY MUCH I AM SURE. BUT I DON'T THINK I OUGHT TO LEAVE MY FRIENDS LIKE THIS, AFTER ALL WE HAVE GONE THROUGH TOGETHER, AND I PROMISED TO WAKE OLD BOMBUR AT MIDNIGHT, TOO! REALLY I MUST BE GOING, AND QUICKLY.
WELL DONE! MISTER BAGGINS! THERE IS ALWAYS MORE ABOUT YOU THAN ANYONE EXPECTS!
GANDALF! I AM SO GLAD TO SEE YOU! WHERE HAVE YOU—
ALL IN GOOD TIME! THINGS ARE DRAWING TOWARDS THE END NOW, UNLESS I AM MISTAKEN. THERE IS AN UNPLEASANT TIME JUST IN FRONT OF YOU; BUT KEEP YOUR HEART UP! YOU *MAY* COME THROUGH ALL RIGHT. THERE IS NEWS BREWING THAT EVEN THE RAVENS HAVE NOT HEARD. GOOD NIGHT!
Puzzled but cheered, Bilbo hurried on. At midnight he woke up Bombur.

About midday the banners of the Forest and the Lake were seen to be borne forth again.
HAIL THORIN! ARE YOU STILL OF THE SAME MIND?
MY MIND DOES NOT CHANGE WITH THE RISING AND SETTING OF A FEW SUNS. DID YOU COME TO ASK ME IDLE QUESTIONS? STILL THE ELF-HOST HAS NOT DEPARTED AS I BADE! TILL THEN YOU COME IN VAIN TO BARGAIN WITH ME.

IS THERE THEN NOTHING FOR WHICH YOU WOULD YIELD ANY OF YOUR GOLD?
WHAT OF THE ARKEN-STONE OF THRAIN?

THAT STONE WAS MY FATHER'S, AND IS MINE. WHY SHOULD I PURCHASE MY OWN?
BUT HOW CAME YOU BY THE HEIRLOOM OF MY HOUSE— IF THERE IS NEED TO ASK SUCH A QUESTION OF THIEVES?
I GAVE IT TO THEM!

YOU! YOU! YOU MISERABLE HOBBIT! YOU UNDERSIZED— BURGLAR! BY THE BEARD OF DURIN! I WISH I HAD GANDALF HERE! CURSE HIM FOR HIS CHOICE OF YOU! MAY HIS BEARD WITHER! AS FOR YOU I WILL THROW YOU TO THE ROCKS!

STAY! YOUR WISH IS GRANTED!
HERE IS GANDALF! AND NONE TOO SOON IT SEEMS. IF YOU DON'T LIKE MY BURGLAR, PLEASE DON'T DAMAGE HIM. PUT HIM DOWN, AND LISTEN FIRST TO WHAT HE HAS TO SAY!

DEAR ME! DEAR ME! YOU MAY REMEMBER SAYING THAT I MIGHT CHOOSE MY OWN FOUR-TEENTH SHARE? PERHAPS I TOOK IT TOO LITERALLY. THE TIME WAS, ALL THE SAME, WHEN YOU SEEMED TO THINK THAT I HAD BEEN OF SOME SERVICE. TAKE IT THAT I HAVE DISPOSED OF MY SHARE AS I WISHED, AND LET IT GO AT THAT?
I WILL.
AND FOR THE ARKENSTONE I WILL GIVE ONE FOURTEENTH SHARE OF THE HOARD IN SILVER AND GOLD; BUT THAT SHALL BE ACCOUNTED THE PROMISED SHARE OF THIS TRAITOR AND YOU CAN DIVIDE IT AS YOU WILL.

BE OFF! YOU HAVE UPON YOU A COAT OF SILVER-STEEL, WHICH THE ELVES CALL MITHRIL, AND IT IS TOO GOOD FOR YOU. IT CANNOT BE PIERCED BY ARROWS; BUT IF YOU DO NOT HASTEN, I WILL STING YOUR MISERABLE FEET.
WHAT ABOUT THE GOLD AND SILVER?
THAT WILL FOLLOW AFTER AS CAN BE ARRANGED.

UNTIL THEN WE KEEP THE STONE. AT NOON TOMORROW WE WILL RETURN, AND SEE IF YOU HAVE BROUGHT FROM THE HOARD THE PORTION THAT IS TO BE SET AGAINST THE STONE. IF THAT IS DONE WITHOUT DECEIT, THEN WE WILL DEPART.
YOU ARE NOT MAKING A VERY SPLENDID FIGURE AS KING UNDER THE MOUN-TAIN. BUT THINGS MAY CHANGE YET.

That day passed and the night. The next morning was still early when a cry was heard in the camp.

Dain had come.

Thorin had sent messengers by Roäc telling Dain of what had passed the day before. And Dain had hurried on through the night, and so had come upon them sooner than expected.

WE ARE SENT FROM DAIN SON OF NAIN. WE ARE HASTENING TO OUR KINSMEN IN THE MOUNTAIN, SINCE WE LEARN THAT THE KINGDOM OF OLD IS RENEWED. BUT WHO ARE YOU THAT SIT IN THE PLAIN AS FOES BEFORE DEFENDED WALLS?

They meant to push on between the Mountain and the loop of the river, for the narrow land there did not seem to be strongly guarded.

Bard, of course, refused to allow the dwarves to go straight on to the Mountain. He was determined to wait until the gold and silver had been brought out in exchange for the Arkenstone. The dwarves had brought with them a great store of supplies. They would stand a siege for weeks, and by that time yet more dwarves might come.

So after angry words, the dwarf-messengers retired, muttering in their beards.

Bard then sent messengers at once to the Gate; but they found no gold or payment. Arrows came forth as soon as they were within shot.

In the camp all was now astir, as if for battle; for the dwarves of Dain were advancing along the eastern bank.

FOOLS! THEY DO NOT UNDERSTAND WAR ABOVE GROUND, WHATEVER THEY MAY KNOW OF BATTLE IN THE MINES. LET US SET ON THEM NOW FROM BOTH SIDES, BEFORE THEY ARE FULLY RESTED.

LONG WILL I TARRY, ERE I BEGIN THIS WAR FOR GOLD. LET US HOPE STILL FOR SOMETHING THAT WILL BRING RECONCILIATION. OUR ADVANTAGE IN NUMBERS WILL BE ENOUGH, IF IN THE END IT MUST COME TO UNHAPPY BLOWS.

But the Elvenking reckoned without the dwarves. The knowledge that the Arkenstone was in the hands of the besiegers burned in their thought.

Suddenly without a signal they sprang silently forward to attack.

Still more suddenly a darkness came on with dreadful swiftness; but it did not come with the wind, it came from the North, like a vast cloud of birds, so dense that no light could be seen between their wings.

HALT!

DREAD HAS COME UPON YOU ALL! THE GOBLINS ARE UPON YOU! BOLG OF THE NORTH IS COMING. BEHOLD! THE BATS ARE ABOVE HIS ARMY LIKE A SEA OF LOCUSTS. THEY RIDE UPON WOLVES AND WARGS ARE IN THEIR TRAIN!

COME! THERE IS YET TIME FOR COUNCIL. LET DAIN SON OF NAIN COME SWIFTLY TO US!

So began a battle that none had expected; and it was called the Battle of Five Armies, and it was very terrible. Upon one side were the Goblins and the wild Wolves, and upon the other were Elves and Men and Dwarves.

Ever since the fall of the Great Goblin of the Misty Mountains the hatred of their race for the dwarves had been rekindled to fury. Messengers had passed to and fro between all their cities, colonies and strongholds; for they resolved now to win the dominion of the North.

Then they learned of the death of Smaug, and joy was in their hearts; and they hastened night after night through the mountains, and came thus at last on a sudden from the North hard on the heels of Dain.

The council's only hope was to lure the goblins into the valley between the arms of the mountain; and themselves to man the great spurs that struck south and east.

Yet this would be perilous, if the goblins were in sufficient numbers to overrun the Mountain itself, and so attack them also from behind and above.

On the Southern spur the Elves were set.

On the Eastern spur were men and dwarves.

Ere long the vanguard swirled round the spur's end and came rushing into Dale. Many brave men fell before the rest drew back and fled to either side.

The goblin banners were countless, black and red, and they came on like a tide in fury and disorder.

It was a terrible battle.
Bilbo put on his ring early in the business, and vanished from sight, if not from all danger. A magic ring of that sort does not stop flying arrows and wild spears; but it prevents your head from being specially chosen for a sweeping stroke by a goblin swordsman.
The elves were the first to charge. Their hatred for the goblins is cold and bitter. They sent against their enemies a shower of arrows, and each flickered as it fled as if with stinging fire. Behind the arrows a thousand of their spearmen leapt down and charged. The rocks were stained black with goblin blood.
Just as the goblins were recovering from the onslaught and the elf-charge was halted, there rose from across the valley a deep-throated roar. With cries of "Moria!" and "Dain, Dain!" the dwarves of the Iron Hills plunged in, wielding their mattocks, upon the other side; and beside them came the men of the Lake with long swords.
Panic came upon the goblins; and even as they turned to meet this new attack, the elves charged again with renewed numbers. Victory seemed at hand, when a cry rang out on the heights above.
Goblins had scaled the Mountain from the other side and already many were on the slopes above the Gate, and others were streaming down recklessly to attack the spurs from above. Victory now vanished from hope. They had only stemmed the first onslaught of the black tide.
Day drew on. The goblins gathered again in the valley. There a host of Wargs came ravening and with them came the bodyguard of Bolg. Now Bard was fighting to defend the Eastern spur, and yet giving slowly back; and the elf-lords were at bay about their king upon the southern arm, near to the watch-post on Ravenhill.
Suddenly there was a great shout, and from the Gate came a trumpet call.

They had forgotten Thorin!

Once again the goblins were stricken in the valley; and they were piled in heaps till Dale was dark and hideous with their corpses. The Wargs were scattered and Thorin drove right against the bodyguards of Bolg.

But he could not pierce their ranks.

As the valley widened his onset grew ever slower. His numbers were too few. His flanks were unguarded. Soon the attackers were attacked, hemmed all about with goblins and wolves returning to the assault. The bodyguard of Bolg came howling against them, and drove in upon their ranks like waves upon cliffs of sand.

On all this Bilbo looked with misery.

IT WILL NOT BE LONG NOW BEFORE THE GOBLINS WIN THE GATE, AND WE ARE ALL SLAUGHTERED OR DRIVEN DOWN AND CAPTURED. REALLY IT IS ENOUGH TO MAKE ONE WEEP, AFTER ALL ONE HAS GONE THROUGH.

I WOULD RATHER OLD SMAUG HAD BEEN LEFT WITH ALL THE WRETCHED TREASURE THAN THAT THESE VILE CREATURES SHOULD GET IT, AND POOR OLD BOMBUR, AND BALIN AND FILI AND KILI AND ALL THE REST COME TO A BAD END.

MISERY ME! I WISH I WAS WELL OUT OF IT.

The clouds were torn by the wind, and a red sunset slashed the West. Seeing the sudden gleam in the gloom Bilbo looked round. He gave a great cry: he had seen a sight that made his heart leap, dark shapes small yet majestic against the distant glow.

The eagles were coming down the wind, line after line in such a host as must have gathered from all the eyries of the North. If the elves could not see Bilbo they could hear him. Soon they too took up the cry, and it echoed across the valley.

At that moment a stone hurtling from above smote heavily on Bilbo's helm...

...and he fell with a crash and knew no more.

When Bilbo came to himself, he was literally by himself. He was shaking and as chilled as stone, but his head burned with fire.
NOW I WONDER WHAT HAS HAPPENED?

VICTORY AFTER ALL, I SUPPOSE!
HELLO THERE! HULLO THERE! WHAT NEWS?
WHAT VOICE IS IT THAT SPEAKS AMONG THE STONES?

WELL I'M BLESSED! THIS INVISIBILITY HAS ITS DRAWBACKS AFTER ALL. OTHERWISE I SUPPOSE I MIGHT HAVE SPENT A WARM AND COMFORTABLE NIGHT IN BED!
IT'S ME, BILBO BAGGINS, COMPANION OF THORIN!

IT IS WELL THAT I HAVE FOUND YOU! YOU ARE NEEDED AND WE HAVE LOOKED FOR YOU LONG. I HAVE BEEN SENT TO LOOK HERE FOR THE LAST TIME.
ARE YOU HURT?
A NASTY KNOCK ON THE HEAD, I THINK, BUT I HAVE A HELM AND A HARD SKULL. ALL THE SAME I FEEL SICK AND MY LEGS ARE LIKE STRAWS.

I WILL CARRY YOU DOWN TO THE CAMP IN THE VALLEY.

BAGGINS! WELL I NEVER! ALIVE AFTER ALL—I AM GLAD! I BEGAN TO WONDER IF EVEN YOUR LUCK WOULD SEE YOU THROUGH! A TERRIBLE BUSINESS, AND IT NEARLY WAS DISASTROUS.
BUT OTHER NEWS CAN WAIT. COME! YOU ARE CALLED FOR.

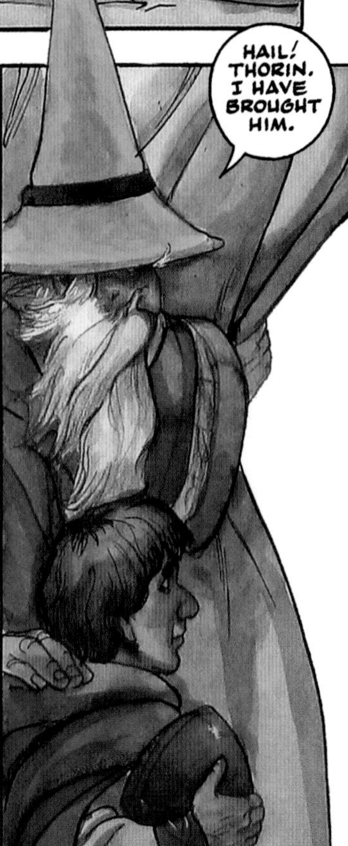
HAIL! THORIN. I HAVE BROUGHT HIM.

FAREWELL, GOOD THIEF. I GO NOW TO THE HALLS OF WAITING TO SIT BESIDE MY FATHERS, UNTIL THE WORLD IS RENEWED.
SINCE I LEAVE NOW ALL GOLD AND SILVER, AND GO WHERE IT IS OF LITTLE WORTH, I WISH TO PART IN FRIENDSHIP FROM YOU, AND I WOULD TAKE BACK MY WORDS AND DEEDS AT THE GATE.
FAREWELL, KING UNDER THE MOUNTAIN! THIS IS A BITTER ADVENTURE IF IT MUST END SO; AND NOT A MOUNTAIN OF GOLD CAN AMEND IT. YET I AM GLAD THAT I HAVE SHARED IN YOUR PERILS—THAT HAS BEEN MORE THAN ANY BAGGINS DESERVES.
NO! THERE IS MORE IN YOU OF GOOD THAN YOU KNOW, CHILD OF THE KINDLY WEST. SOME COURAGE AND SOME WISDOM, BLENDED IN MEASURE. IF MORE OF US VALUED FOOD AND CHEER AND SONG ABOVE HOARDED GOLD, IT WOULD BE A MERRIER WORLD.
BUT SAD OR MERRY, I MUST LEAVE IT NOW. FAREWELL!
Then Bilbo turned away, and he went by himself, and sat alone, and, whether you believe it or not, he wept until his eyes were red and his voice was hoarse. He was a kindly little soul. Indeed it was long before he had the heart to make a joke again.
A MERCY IT IS THAT I WOKE UP WHEN I DID. I WISH THORIN WERE LIVING, BUT I AM GLAD THAT WE PARTED IN KINDNESS.
YOU ARE A FOOL, BILBO BAGGINS, AND YOU MADE A GREAT MESS OF THAT BUSINESS WITH THE STONE; AND THERE WAS A BATTLE, IN SPITE OF ALL YOUR EFFORTS TO BUY PEACE AND QUIET, BUT I SUPPOSE YOU CAN HARDLY BE BLAMED FOR THAT.

All that had happened after he was stunned Bilbo learned later.

The Eagles had long had suspicion of the goblins' mustering. So they too had gathered in great numbers; and at length smelling battle from afar they had come speeding down the gale in the nick of time. They it was who dislodged the goblins from the mountainslopes.

But even with the Eagles they were still outnumbered. In that last hour Beorn himself had appeared—no one knew how or from where. He came alone, and in bear's shape; and he seemed to have grown almost to giant-size in his wrath.

He fell upon their rear, and broke like a clap of thunder through the ring. Then Beorn stooped and lifted Thorin, who had fallen pierced with spears, and bore him out of the fray.

Swiftly he returned and his wrath was redoubled, so that nothing could withstand him, and no weapon seemed to bite him. He scattered the bodyguard, and pulled down Bolg himself and crushed him.
Then dismay fell on the Goblins and they fled in all directions. But weariness left their enemies with the coming of new hope, and they pursued them closely, and prevented most of them from escaping where they could.
Songs have said that three parts of the goblin warriors of the North perished on that day, and the mountains had peace for many a year.
WHERE ARE THE EAGLES?

SOME ARE IN THE HUNT, BUT MOST HAVE GONE BACK TO THEIR EYRIES.
THEY WOULD NOT STAY HERE, AND DEPARTED WITH THE FIRST LIGHT OF MORNING. DAIN HAS CROWNED THEIR CHIEF WITH GOLD, AND SWORN FRIENDSHIP WITH THEM FOREVER.
I AM SORRY, I MEAN, I SHOULD HAVE LIKED TO SEE THEM AGAIN. PERHAPS I SHALL SEE THEM ON THE WAY HOME.

I SUPPOSE I SHALL BE GOING HOME SOON?

AS SOON AS YOU LIKE.

Actually it was some days before Bilbo really set out. They buried Thorin deep beneath the Mountain, and Bard laid the Arkenstone upon his breast.
THERE LET IT LIE TILL THE MOUNTAIN FALLS; MAY IT BRING GOOD FORTUNE TO ALL HIS FOLD THAT DWELL HERE AFTER!

Upon his tomb the Elvenking then laid Orcrist, the elvish sword that had been taken from Thorin in captivity. It is said in songs that it gleamed ever in the dark if foes approached, and the fortress of the dwarves could not be taken by surprise.

There now Dain son of Nain took up his abode, and he became King under the Mountain.

Of the twelve companions of Thorin, ten remained. Fili and Kili had fallen defending him with shield and body, for he was their mother's elder brother.

WE WILL HONOUR THE AGREEMENT OF THE DEAD AND HE HAS NOW THE ARKENSTONE IN HIS KEEPING.

There was, of course, no longer any question of dividing the hoard in such shares as had been planned. Yet a fourteenth share of all the silver and gold, wrought and unwrought, was given up to Bard. From that treasure Bard sent much gold to the Master of Laketown. To the Elvenking he gave the emeralds of Girion which Dain had restored to him.

THIS TREASURE IS AS MUCH YOURS AS IT IS MINE. YET EVEN THOUGH YOU WERE WILLING TO LAY ASIDE ALL YOUR CLAIM, I SHOULD WISH THAT THE WORDS OF THORIN, OF WHICH HE REPENTED, SHOULD NOT PROVE TRUE; THAT WE SHOULD GIVE YOU LITTLE. I WOULD REWARD YOU MOST RICHLY OF ALL.
VERY KIND OF YOU. BUT REALLY IT IS A RELIEF TO ME. HOW ON EARTH SHOULD I HAVE GOT ALL THAT TREASURE HOME WITHOUT WAR AND MURDER ALL ALONG THE WAY, I DON'T KNOW. I AM SURE IT IS BETTER IN YOUR HANDS.

In the end he would only take two small chests, one filled with silver, and the other with gold. "That will be quite as much as I can manage," said he.
FAREWELL, BALIN! AND FAREWELL, DWALIN! AND FAREWELL DORI, NORI, ORI, OIN, GLOIN, BIFUR, BOFUR, AND BOMBUR! MAY YOUR BEARDS NEVER GROW THIN!
FAREWELL, THORIN OAKENSHIELD! AND FILI AND KILI! MAY YOUR MEMORY NEVER FADE!

GOOD-BYE AND GOOD LUCK, WHEREVER YOU FARE! IF EVER YOU VISIT US AGAIN, WHEN OUR HALLS ARE MADE FAIR ONCE MORE, THE FEAST SHALL INDEED BE SPLENDID!
IF EVER YOU ARE PASSING MY WAY, DON'T WAIT TO KNOCK! TEA IS AT FOUR! BUT ANY OF YOU ARE WELCOME AT ANY TIME!

The elf-host was on the march; and if it was sadly lessened, yet many were glad, for the dragon was dead, and the goblins overthrown, and their hearts looked forward after winter to a spring of joy.

So they went on until they drew near to the borders of Mirkwood. Then they halted, for the wizard and Bilbo intended to go along the edge of the forest, and round its northern end. It was a long and cheerless road, but now that the goblins were crushed, it seemed safer to them than the dreadful pathways under the trees. Moreover Beorn was going that way too.
FAREWELL! O ELVENKING! MERRY BE THE GREENWOOD, WHILE THE WORLD IS YET YOUNG.
AND MERRY BE YOUR FOLK!
FAREWELL! O GANDALF! MAY YOU EVER APPEAR WHERE YOU ARE MOST NEEDED AND LEAST EXPECTED! THE OFTENER YOU APPEAR IN MY HALLS THE BETTER SHALL I BE PLEASED!
I BEG OF YOU TO ACCEPT THIS GIFT!
IN WHAT WAY HAVE I EARNED SUCH A GIFT, O HOBBIT?
WELL, er, I THOUGHT, DON'T YOU KNOW THAT, er, SOME LITTLE RETURN SHOULD BE MADE FOR YOUR, er, HOSPITALITY. I HAVE DRUNK MUCH OF YOUR WINE AND EATEN MUCH OF YOUR BREAD.

I WILL TAKE YOUR GIFT, O BILBO THE MAGNIFICENT! AND I NAME YOU ELF-FRIEND AND BLESSED. MAY YOUR SHADOW NEVER GROW LESS (OR STEALING WOULD BE TOO EASY)! FAREWELL!

Bilbo had many hardships and adventures before he got back. The Wild was still the Wild, and there were many other things in it in those days—besides goblins.
Anyway by mid-winter Gandalf and Bilbo had come all the way back to the doors of Beorn's house; and there for a while they both stayed.
Beorn became a great chief afterwards in those regions; and it is said that for many generations the men of his line had the power of taking bear's shape.

It was spring before Bilbo and Gandalf took their leave at last of Beorn, and at last they came up the long road, and reached the very pass where the goblins had captured them before. There far away was the Lonely Mountain on the edge of eyesight, On its highest peak snow yet unmelted was gleaming pale.
SO COMES SNOW AFTER FIRE, AND EVEN DRAGONS HAVE THEIR ENDING!
I WISH NOW ONLY TO BE IN MY OWN ARM-CHAIR!

It was on May the First that the two came back at last to the brink of the valley of Rivendell, where stood the Last (or the First) Homely House.

There a warm welcome was made them, and there were many eager ears that evening to hear the tale of their adventures.

Gandalf it was who spoke, for Bilbo was fallen quite drowsy. It was in this way that Bilbo learned where Gandalf had been to.

It appeared that Gandalf had been to a great council of the white wizards, masters of lore and good magic; and that they had at last driven the Necromancer from his dark hold in the south of Mirkwood.

ERE LONG NOW THE FOREST WILL GROW SOMEWHAT MORE WHOLESOME. THE NORTH WILL BE FREED FROM THAT HORROR FOR MANY LONG YEARS, I HOPE. YET I WISH HE WERE BANISHED FROM THE WORLD!

IT WOULD BE WELL INDEED, BUT I FEAR THAT WILL NOT COME ABOUT IN THIS AGE OF THE WORLD, OR FOR MANY AFTER.

Weariness fell from Bilbo soon in that house. Yet even that place could not long delay him now, and he thought always of his own home. After a week, therefore, he said farewell to Elrond, and giving him such small gifts as he would accept, he rode away with Gandalf.

MERRY IS MAY-TIME! BUT OUR BACK IS TO LEGENDS AND WE ARE COMING HOME. I SUPPOSE THIS IS A FIRST TASTE OF IT.
THERE IS A LONG ROAD YET.
BUT IT IS THE LAST ROAD.

At each point on the road Bilbo recalled the happenings and the words of a year ago—it seemed to him more like ten—so that, of course, he quickly noted the place where they had turned aside for their nasty adventure with Tom and Bert and Bill.

Not far from the road they found the gold of the trolls, which they had buried, still hidden and untouched.
I HAVE ENOUGH TO LAST ME MY TIME. YOU HAD BETTER TAKE THIS, GANDALF. I DARESAY YOU CAN FIND A USE FOR IT.
INDEED I CAN! BUT SHARE AND SHARE ALIKE! YOU MAY FIND YOU HAVE MORE NEEDS THAN YOU EXPECT.

After that their going was slower, for most of the time they walked. But the land was green and there was much grass through which the hobbit strolled along contentedly—for now June had brought summer, and the weather was bright and hot again.

As all things come to an end, even this story, a day came at last when Bilbo could see his own Hill in the distance.
ROADS GO EVER EVER ON
UNDER CLOUD AND UNDER STAR,
YET FEET THAT WANDERING HAVE GONE
TURN AT LAST TO HOME AFAR.
EYES THAT FOREST AND FIRE HAVE SEEN
AND HORROR IN THE HALLS OF STONE
LOOK AT LAST ON MEADOWS GREEN
AND TREES AND HILLS THEY LONG HAVE KNOWN

MY DEAR BILBO! SOMETHING IS THE MATTER WITH YOU! YOU ARE NOT THE HOBBIT THAT YOU WERE.

BLESS ME! WHAT'S GOING ON?
Bilbo had arrived back in the middle of an auction! There was a large notice in black and red hung on the gate, stating that on June the Twenty-second Messers. Grubb, Grubb, and Burrowes would sell by auction the effects of the late Bilbo Baggins Esquire, of Bag-End, Underhill, Hobbiton. Sale to commence at ten o'clock sharp.
AUCTION

It was now nearly lunchtime, and most of the things had already been sold, for various prices from next to nothing to old songs (as is not unusual at auction).

Bilbo's cousins the Sackvill-Bagginses were, in fact, busy measuring his rooms to see if their own furniture would fit. In short Bilbo was "Presumed Dead," and not everybody that said so was sorry to find the presumption wrong.

The return of Mr. Bilbo Baggins created quite a disturbance, both under the Hill and over the Hill, and across the Water; it was a great deal more than a nine days' wonder. The legal bother, indeed, lasted for years.

In the end to save time Bilbo had to buy back quite a lot of his own furniture. Many of his silver spoons mysteriously disappeared and were never accounted for.

Indeed Bilbo found he had lost more than spoons—he had lost his reputation. It is true that for ever after he remained an elf-friend, and had the honour of dwarves, wizards, and all such folk as ever passed that way; but he was no longer quite respectable.

He was in fact held by all the hobbits of the neighbourhood to be 'queer'—except by his nephews and nieces on the Took side, but even they were not encouraged in their friendship by their elders.

I am sorry to say he did not mind. He was quite content. His sword he hung over the mantlepiece. His coat of mail was arranged on a stand in the hall (until he lent it to a Museum). His gold and silver was largely spent in presents. His magic ring he kept a great secret, for he chiefly used it when unpleasant callers came.

He took to writing poetry and visiting the elves; and though few believed any of his tales, he remained very happy to the end of his days, and those were extraordinarily long.

One autumn evening some years afterwards Bilbo was sitting in his study writing his memoirs—he thought of calling them "There and Back Again, a Hobbit's Holiday"—when there was a ring at the door.
It was Gandalf and a dwarf; and the dwarf was actually Balin.
COME IN! COME IN!
Soon they fell to talking of their times together, of course, and Bilbo asked how things were going in the lands of the Mountain. It seemed they were going well.
Bard had rebuilt the town in Dale and all the valley had become tilled again and rich, and the desolation was now filled with birds and blossoms in spring and fruit and feasting in autumn.
And Lake-town was refounded and was more prosperous than ever, and much wealth went up and down the Running River; and there was friendship in those parts between elves and dwarves and men.
THE NEW MASTER IS OF WISER KIND AND VERY POPULAR, FOR, OF COURSE, HE GETS MOST OF THE CREDIT FOR THE PRESENT PROSPERITY. THEY ARE MAKING SONGS WHICH SAY THAT IN HIS DAY THE RIVERS RUN WITH GOLD.
The old Master had come to a bad end. Bard had given him much gold for the help of the Lake-people, but being of the kind that easily catches such disease he fell under the dragon-sickness, and took most of the gold and fled with it, and died of starvation in the Waste, deserted by his companions.
THEN THE PROPHECIES OF THE OLD SONGS HAVE TURNED OUT TO BE TRUE, AFTER A FASHION!
OF COURSE! AND WHY SHOULD NOT THEY PROVE TRUE?
SURELY YOU DON'T DISBELIEVE THE PROPHECIES, BECAUSE YOU HAD A HAND IN BRINGING THEM ABOUT YOURSELF? YOU DON'T REALLY SUPPOSE, DO YOU, THAT ALL YOUR ADVENTURES AND ESCAPES WERE MANAGED BY MERE LUCK, JUST FOR YOUR SOLE BENEFIT?
YOU ARE A VERY FINE PERSON, MISTER BAGGINS, AND I AM FOND OF YOU; BUT YOU ARE ONLY QUITE A LITTLE FELLOW IN A WIDE WORLD AFTER ALL!
THANK GOODNESS!
The End

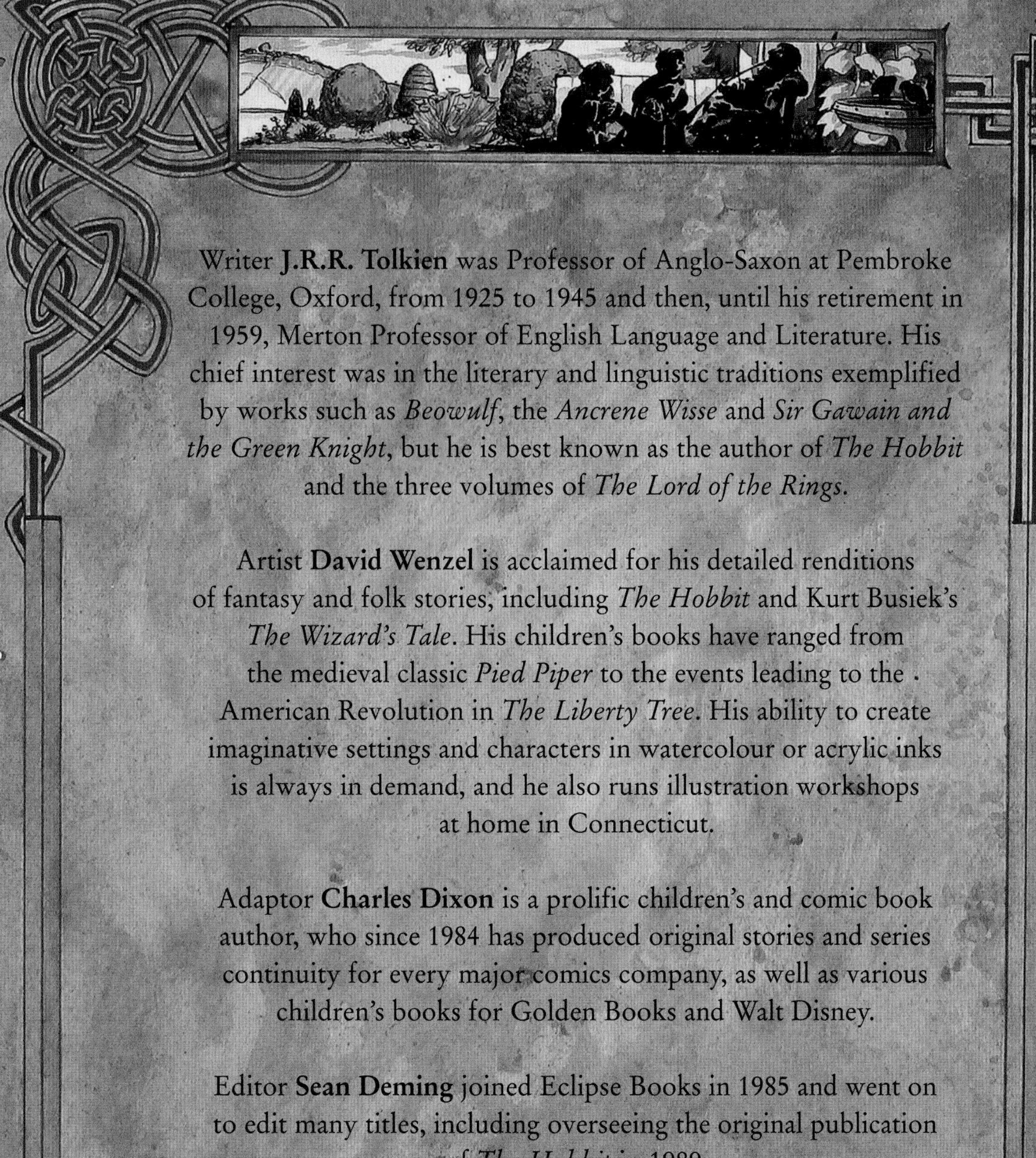

Writer **J.R.R. Tolkien** was Professor of Anglo-Saxon at Pembroke College, Oxford, from 1925 to 1945 and then, until his retirement in 1959, Merton Professor of English Language and Literature. His chief interest was in the literary and linguistic traditions exemplified by works such as *Beowulf*, the *Ancrene Wisse* and *Sir Gawain and the Green Knight*, but he is best known as the author of *The Hobbit* and the three volumes of *The Lord of the Rings*.

Artist **David Wenzel** is acclaimed for his detailed renditions of fantasy and folk stories, including *The Hobbit* and Kurt Busiek's *The Wizard's Tale*. His children's books have ranged from the medieval classic *Pied Piper* to the events leading to the American Revolution in *The Liberty Tree*. His ability to create imaginative settings and characters in watercolour or acrylic inks is always in demand, and he also runs illustration workshops at home in Connecticut.

Adaptor **Charles Dixon** is a prolific children's and comic book author, who since 1984 has produced original stories and series continuity for every major comics company, as well as various children's books for Golden Books and Walt Disney.

Editor **Sean Deming** joined Eclipse Books in 1985 and went on to edit many titles, including overseeing the original publication of *The Hobbit* in 1989.

Letterer **Bill Pearson** had written, edited, coloured, illustrated and lettered comics for 30 years before *The Hobbit*. At a time when hand-lettering is a dying art, this book is a perfect example of how the skilful use of letter forms can enhance the overall design.